THE HEIR OF WINTER

THE DRAGONS OF FIRE AND ICE
BOOK FOUR

AMELIA SHAW

ONE

DYMITRI

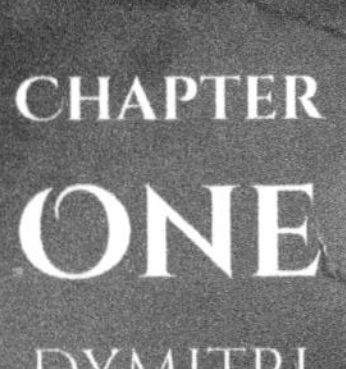

In the blink of an eye, everything had changed. One minute, I was sitting awkwardly in the royal hall of my ancestors, hardly able to believe our reversal of fortune. The next, my brother and I were told that our fated mates were *human* women.

That would have been enough of a surprise. My brother and I had always assumed that we didn't have fated mates. Only the luckiest of shifters enjoyed that privilege.

But the real shock came when Marienne told us that these women—these strangers—were in danger. She said we had to fly to the human realm immediately and save them, before they were lost forever.

My brother and I shifted into our dragons and launched off the palace balcony into the air. We followed King Stavrok, who had agreed to accompany us. We'd never been south of our kingdom, let alone to another world. But our mates needed us, so we didn't hesitate. Though the fear and trepidation that pulsed through my heart was very real indeed.

The cold air nipped at my face as we flew closer to the magical barrier that divided my world from the human realm, with no idea of what lay waiting on the other side.

We were dizzyingly high already, but we kept climbing. The air was thinner up here; there were no birds, nothing around us but thin strands of cloud. Beside me, my brother's wings beat hard, but he managed to keep pace as we followed Stavrok to the portal.

Lucian and I had always pushed each other, spurred each other on with every challenge. We'd always competed fiercely. It was what had enabled us to survive all these years of exile out in the wilderness.

But we weren't alone anymore. Our half-brother, King Damon, had agreed to take us in and allow our people to live within the safety of the kingdom's walls. But even more so, Damon had asked us to live in the castle with him. That had changed our lives in many ways. Especially now. Without his contacts we would never have met the sorceress who had given us a glimpse into our future. With our mates.

Stavrok let out a puff of fire when we reached the barrier as a signal to us. I slowed, flapping my wings hard and stared at the space before us. It was little more than a ripple in the air. The faint golden color would have been easy to miss if you weren't looking for it.

Lucian pulled up next to me, hovering in mid-air.

Stavrok went through first, disappearing into oblivion. I swallowed my fear and, after a glance at my brother, I followed, slipping through the portal after Stavrok.

I inhaled sharply when I emerged.

The change in the air was stark. In our world, a cold wind had been blasting over the frozen tundra of the north. But here it was warmer. Even the sky was different: a pale, peach color in the glow of the setting sun.

Stavrok circled down to earth below me, but I waited for my brother.

When Lucian flew through the portal and appeared at my shoulder, a sense of relief and happiness swept over me. I could tell from Lucian's expression that he felt the same. We'd made it through unharmed.

We fell into a simultaneous dive in perfect sync, wings spiraling outwards. It was a neat trick—impressive, according to those who had seen it in the past. We'd been doing it since we were kids. We didn't need a signal. In the air, our shifters could practically read each other's minds.

We landed in the middle of a cornfield, and I found myself panting for breath. We were ice dragons. We breathed ice, not fire. And we weren't as used to this warmth as Stavrok.

The king was waiting for us, hands on his now-human hips. He gestured toward a small farmhouse to show us where we would be going next.

I glanced at my brother, and together, we let go of our shifters and became human once more. Naked humans, like Stavrok after his shift. Would this be an issue, here in the human world?

As if he'd read my mind, Stavrok said, "These people are loyal to our kind. They will clothe us and provide some means of transport."

"All right." I nodded at the king. We had to trust him, but everything in me was tense and on guard. I was ready to shift back and launch into the air at a moment's notice.

This was not our world and nothing about this situation felt natural.

I followed Stavrok, together with Lucian, without voicing the questions that were shouting inside my head. Judging by his relaxed body language, Stavrok wasn't worried about the fact that we had all arrived naked in the middle of a field.

But, I couldn't help the nerves that ran through me. When I

looked at Lucian, he seemed equally tense: jaw tightly clenched, hands held in fists at his side.

We stepped out of the field and walked toward the farmhouse.

Lucian and I hung back while Stavrok rapped on the door. I had no idea what to expect, but a small buxom woman who seemed glad to see us, was not on my list.

"Come in, come in. Out of the cold," she said, and ushered us into a small cloakroom. "Help yourself to anything that will fit you."

The woman looked at Stavrok with the kind of reverence I wasn't expecting from a human.

When we were left alone to dress, I grabbed Stavrok's arm. "Do they know about us? About you being one of our dragon kings?"

Her behavior didn't make sense with any other explanation.

"Yes. This family guards the entrance to the human world." He pulled on a pair of slacks designed to fit a man with his large frame.

These people were obviously accustomed to our size as I found clothes that fit me perfectly well, even though I'd heard that the men in this realm tended to be smaller in stature than our kind.

"I have been meaning to return here for some time," Stavrok went on. "They did me a great kindness when I came here to find Lucy."

I spared a glance at Lucian, who was buttoning his shirt with clumsy fingers. There was a frown on his face and I knew that look too well. He hadn't spoken since we arrived, which didn't surprise me. He was always the more stoic one of us. I was used to doing the talking.

When we stepped back into the main living area of the small house, the woman had returned with a man in tow. He had the look of a farmer. Although he was much shorter than us, he was stocky and strong-looking. His eyes darted between the three of us and in contrast to the wife, it seemed like he couldn't wait for us to leave.

"There's a car waiting for you out front." The woman smiled at us as she spoke, digging around in her pocket before pulling out a wad of cash and handing it to Stavrok. "This should be enough, Sire. Please call us if you need anything else."

Stavrok bent his head and kissed the woman's hand, making her giggle. "I thank you. I will return when we find what we're looking for."

The woman's gaze fell on my brother and me, and her eyes softened. I wasn't sure how much she knew, but I felt warmed by her kindness, nonetheless.

"Good luck," she said, waving as we left her small home and went on our way.

"Forgive me," Stavrok said as he jammed the gearstick into position with a crunch. "It's been many years since I've driven a car."

"Don't worry about it," I said between clenched teeth as we rumbled over a pothole. The bump lurched the car down and sideways. My fingers tightened around the edges of the seat. In the rear-view mirror, Lucian was looking distinctly green. "My brother and I aren't used to them either."

That was an understatement. We'd lived our whole lives in the wilds of the north; for the most part, such modes of transport were totally foreign. We were aware that vehicles like existed, but this was the first time I had actually seen one, let alone dared to ride inside one.

My heart hammered in my chest like I was being chased by a wolf.

Thankfully, the ride became smoother once we reached a main road that widened out into two carriageways. Stavrok's driving became less frantic, which gave me the chance to absorb our surroundings, rather than fearing for my life.

I stared in fascination at the strange markings on the surface of the road, and the giant metal signs that hung overhead.

"Which way?" Stavrok looked in the rear-vision mirror at Lucian when we reached the first intersection.

Marienne the sorceress had put the directions inside Lucian's mind back at the castle. Wordlessly, my brother pointed to the right.

This happened a few more times, and soon enough we were on the outskirts of a city. It was like nothing I'd ever seen before. There were bright, multicolored lights everywhere and pavements full of bustling people and glittering storefronts. As the lights faded outside the car, I didn't know which way to look.

Stavrok tapping his fingers impatiently against the steering wheel was a constant reminder of our mission. The traffic around us was thick, but we snaked through the crowded streets.

I'd never given much thought to who my mate could be. My life up until very recently had been one of survival. Harsh winters and brutal raids had left little time for pleasure, and women had been few and far between.

Some had come and gone over the years. People drifted through our small clan of outlaws, tagging along for a season before disappearing again. They'd warmed my bed, that was all. No woman had left her mark on my heart, and as far as I knew, I hadn't left mine on any, either.

I stared grimly out the window at the blur of lights. Night was falling, and fast.

I glanced at Lucian out of the corner of my eye. I was accustomed to reading his stoic expression, but right now I had no idea what he was thinking.

From what the sorceress Marienne had told us, there would be trouble when we reached our destination. We could hold our own in any battle when we knew the terrain, but this was unfamiliar territory on every level. I'd never fought against humans before.

But I knew in my bones, even though the shock of the revelation had yet to wear off, that I would do anything to protect my mate. Even though I hadn't met her yet.

My mate... I shook my head. As the bastard son of the northern king, thrown out of the kingdom a long time ago, the last thing I ever expected to find, was a human fated mate. I didn't feel worthy, or deserving of such a gift.

It was late evening by the time we left the city behind.

At Lucian's instructions, Stavrok turned down a dark, winding country lane. Then we were once again bumping over potholes and loose stones, the car rumbling as it crept forward.

Stavrok dipped the headlights as we approached so hopefully they wouldn't see us coming.

I couldn't see much outside thanks to the darkness of night. The vague shapes of trees loomed ahead.

I stared hard and through the gaps in the undergrowth, I made out a handful of small outbuildings. Once we cleared the trees, a small yard lay in front of a seemingly empty farmhouse.

"Are you sure this is the right place?" I muttered to Lucian. It looked like no-one had lived here in a long time.

Lucian nodded, his expression grim.

Stavrok shut off the engine and we climbed out of the vehicle.

The wind whistled around the seemingly abandoned dwelling as we approached. Our footsteps echoed loudly in the silence. As we grew closer, the sense of foreboding increased. Something didn't feel right about this place. It was so still and quiet, and yet...

All the windows were boarded up with planks of wood. Why would they need to do that if it was abandoned?

Then I saw it. A thin strip of light beneath the doorway. Stavrok caught the direction of my gaze and nodded before pressing a finger to his lips. I took my place on the other side of the doorway to Lucian.

In one blow, Stavrok shouldered open the door. Light spilled out, along with a gust of warmth and a clatter of surprise from the inhabitants inside.

Crates bound in packing tape were piled around the edges of the room. In the center lay a long table under a single, bare light-bulb, around which a small group of women sat, huddled together. Their eyes were wide with fear. They were all thin, and their hollowed cheeks spoke of weeks of untold suffering.

Clear plastic bags littered the table, along with powder and cutting tools.

Human drugs, then.

I couldn't focus on any of it. Like a fishhook in my gut, my attention was yanked elsewhere.

I almost fell to my knees with the force of the call coming from somewhere inside the house. My hand clamped around Stavrok's shoulder. In normal circumstances, I would never dare touch a king in such a way.

But these weren't normal circumstances.

"She's here," I said with a pained breath. "Somewhere else. Not in this room."

"Are you sure?" Stavrok asked.

I closed my eyes briefly, trying to block out the overwhelming force of the siren song that had led us here. It still threatened to bring me to my knees.

I forced myself to nod. "Yes."

My gaze roved the frightened faces. But there was no flicker of recognition among them. There was only terror staring back.

"She's not in here." I fought to keep the rising panic out of my voice. "But she's close. I can feel it."

I caught Lucian's eye. I don't know what I expected to find. A reflection of my own feelings, perhaps? If my mate was somewhere close by, then my brother's mate was likely with her. But there was no trace of a reaction on his face—only concern.

I dragged my gaze back to the room at large.

"Who's in charge here?" I called, addressing the women.

Silence greeted my words.

Beside me, Stavrok stepped forward. "We do not seek to harm you. We are here to help. Tell us—are there more of you? Are there others being held captive in this place?"

Slowly, one of the women looked up. Her pale face was fraught with anxiety, but she didn't look as spaced out as the others.

She met Stavrok's eye bravely. "There's a basement beneath the house."

She pointed to the corner of the room. My eyes followed her gesture, and a heated pulse shot through me as my eyes landed on a door.

By now, I could hear faint voices coming from another part of the building. They were low and rough—it sounded like a group of men.

A door slammed and the woman who had spoken jerked upright. "They're coming. You have to hurry!"

Stavrok strode toward the source of the male voices. I remained in the center of the room, paralyzed by the flow of hormones that raced through my body. Lucian seemed to sense my altered state, because he took charge, rushing to the front door and beckoning the women forward. They drifted uncertainly toward him, heading out into the darkness.

"There's a car parked in the yard out front. Keys are in the ignition," Lucian told the leader of the women.

I eyed her threadbare clothes and frail physique with worry, but she nodded fiercely at his words.

"Head for the main road."

With whispered thanks, the women slipped off into the night. The car's engine started up just as the door on the other side of the room slammed open.

Stavrok let out an almighty, inhuman roar, and immediately shifted into his dragon form.

A pulse of fury sparked through my chest when I laid eyes on the monsters who'd held these women prisoner. The rage on their faces lasted for only a second before terror replaced it. Bright, hot flames reflected in their eyes as Stavrok released a jet of fire that annihilated the nearest packing crate, reducing it to ashes.

The men turned tail and fled the scene, leaving Stavrok to obliterate the entire room.

"I'll check for stragglers," Lucian yelled over the roar of the flames. "You get to the basement."

As shifters, my brother and I were impervious to the fire that raged around us, but that wouldn't be the case for any humans left behind.

Stavrok came to a halt beside me and shifted back into his human form. His chest heaved with anger.

"Let us finish this." He growled, nodding with narrowed eyes at the door in the corner of the room.

Lucian appeared in the empty doorway, the back rooms still smoldering away behind him. "All clear."

Before any of us could do anything, a dirty, ragged arm appeared through another doorway, followed by the hulking form of a man. His face was twisted with fury as he pointed a gun at Stavrok.

The shot rang out. Stavrok recoiled from the impact. My blood ran cold as I started towards him. I braced the king against my side before he could sink to the floor.

No, no...

With a swift, merciless movement, Lucian raced forward and

snapped the human's neck. He fell to the floor, lifeless, and Lucian turned to us with the same blank, calm expression I'd seen hundreds of times before.

"It's a mere flesh wound." Stavrok shrugged me off, staggering backwards. Sure enough, the bullet had pierced through his shoulder; dark blood ran from the hole in his bare skin. He didn't seem bothered, though, merely shocked that such a thing could happen. "I'll be fine. We must get to the basement."

I didn't need telling twice. Leaving Lucian and Stavrok behind, I hurried to the door in the corner of the room.

My mate was on the other side.

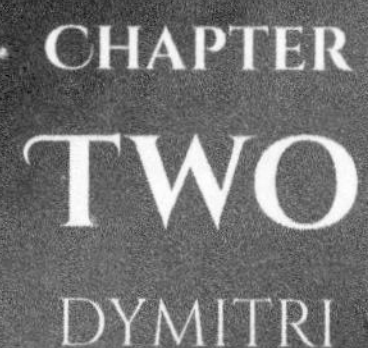

· CHAPTER ·

TWO

DYMITRI

The door was locked when I tried the knob. As if that would stop me. I took a step back, lifted my leg and kicked it in. The door was flimsy and once partly open, I twisted it off its hinges and tossed it aside. A dark stairwell lay beyond the door.

At the bottom of the darkness, a faint light buzzed on the side of the wall—a meager lightbulb illuminating the crooked stairs and peeling walls.

With the door out of the way, the call grew even stronger. It was almost deafening, buzzing through every cell in my body.

I descended the stairs two at a time, landing at the bottom with a grunt. As I straightened, my breath caught in my throat.

Two women were chained up against the far wall. One of them sat slumped over. The small movements of her chest were the only sign of life; she was deathly pale, and her hands lay limply by her sides.

The other one had gotten to her feet at my arrival. Despite her obvious weakness, along with the heavy shackles that bound her wrists and ankles, she stood half in front of the other woman as if to protect her, a determined glare on her face.

"Who are you?"

Her voice was low and rasping, perhaps from dehydration. Even so, the sound was music to my ears. Her words soothed the ache in my chest. I didn't know how long the pained feeling had been there, but it felt like forever.

I took a half-step forward. This was the one. This was my human mate.

Her hand shot outwards, the handcuff clinking around her thin wrist. "Don't come any closer!"

I froze on the spot. The need for her was inside me, building. It was burning hotter and hotter—and I didn't know what to do to ease it.

Stavrok and Lucian came down the stairs more slowly than me, and stopped just behind me. The spell was broken, though, their sudden presence forcing me into action.

The shift began inside me before I could stop it. I couldn't control what was happening even though I fought it. *Now is not the time.* But my dragon would not listen. My vision blurred and I stumbled to my knees, the familiar sensation taking over my body.

As I straightened, my head now hit the low ceiling. My mate gaped up at me. She was glued to the spot, still hovering over the other woman. I let out a snarl and lashed out with my claws, breaking open the chains that bound her in place. She backed away from me, but I advanced on her, grabbing her around the waist and hauling her toward me.

I could feel the tension in her human body as she tried to resist. I realized she was saying something—*pleading*.

"Take me, but please, please—don't hurt my sister! I'll do anything you want—I swear, just let her go!"

Lucian rushed forward and crouched down beside the unconscious girl. He pressed a hand against her forehead, brushing back her hair. He didn't seem affected by her at all, though his actions were possibly gentler than I would normally expect from him. Despite my haze of euphoria, my brain registered his response as strange.

But I couldn't focus on that. My only priority was the woman I held in my grasp.

When she saw Lucian reach for her sister, her thrashing intensified. *"Please!"*

"Get them back to the castle!" Stavrok roared from behind us.

Lucian jumped up and shifted, grabbing the other woman up in his claws. I arched my head back and blasted the ceiling above us with a cold jet of ice. The wooden beams broke apart, shattering in a spectacular fashion and raining debris down on us.

I bent my head and folded my wings over my mate, feeling bits of wood fall onto my wings as I waited for the collapse to finish.

When the area calmed, I looked up once more. The ceiling was gone, leaving the dark, clear night sky beyond open to our flight.

The woman sagged against me. I glanced down. Her eyes had closed. The shock of the roof caving in above us must have been too much for her to handle.

The need was stirring within me, fierce and uncontrollable. I had to get this woman to safety, to take her far away from this place. Back to my home, where I could protect her.

"Tell Lucy I will return to our castle." Stavrok's voice rumbled through the wreckage. He was pulling more rubble down from the hole in the ceiling, making sure the gap was large enough for us to fly through. "I have to take care of things here first."

As if suddenly remembering he was wounded, he pressed a hand against his shoulder. "Tell her our doctors will attend me. She'll worry otherwise."

Lucian launched himself into the sky. I watched his silhouette against the stars, the dark trees framing his steadily shrinking form as he rose.

With one final, parting glance at Stavrok, I followed Lucian into the sky.

~

THE JOURNEY back to the portal between worlds was brief compared to the long, winding car ride from the farmhouse.

Human roads seemed to be full of traffic and pointless diversions. The sky, in comparison, was a vast and mostly empty expanse that we were able to traverse quickly. Our only company was the strange metallic machines covered with blinking lights—the humans' airplanes. Because we were carrying human women, we had to fly far lower than those airplanes, instead of high above them where we would normally choose to travel.

At the altitudes Lucian, Stavrok and I normally flew, these women would not be able to breathe.

It made things slightly trickier on the way back to the portal. We had to fly extra-fast, to avoid detection from the humans below us and ensure that anyone seeing us would have to rub their eyes and look twice. By the time they did that, we'd have been long gone.

My wings beat through the sky until they ached. I pushed on, faster, inhaling deep lungfuls of the cold night air. My blood was burning, my fear for the woman I carried greater than anything I'd ever known.

I didn't know any humans. The only one I had met was Stavrok's wife, Queen Lucy, and I'd hardly said two words to her. I'd certainly never spoken with her properly.

I had no idea how strong they were, or how much trauma their bodies could withstand before they just gave up. What if I hurt the one thing I was destined to protect? What if I accidently *killed* her?

As the thought passed through my mind, I let out a roar into the night sky. The sound shot through the clouds way above us, the icy flames jetting from my mouth and lighting up the surrounding sky like a bolt of lightning.

I couldn't live with myself if anything happened to my mate.

It was a wild shock to me, how quickly everything had changed.

Ever since my brother and I had been welcomed into Damon's castle, our lives had been turned upside down. He had accepted us as his kin, his half-brothers—royalty in our own right. After all these years of scavenging and raids, warfare and the constant, desperate struggle for survival, it was strange to feel as if we had finally been allowed to come home.

But as tough as those exile years had been, at least I'd known my purpose in life. The last few weeks had been amazing... but I was adrift. I'd had no idea what I was supposed to do.

Now? Now I *knew*.

It had been just as the sorceress Marienne had said. My future was in my grasp. My path lay ahead of me. This woman clutched in my talons was the answer to everything.

Now, all that was left was to protect her. Cherish her. And claim her for myself.

When we finally made it to the shimmering air around the portal, I exhaled with relief. We were almost home.

How I longed to set foot on our home turf once again. The sky changed when we passed through the gateway between the worlds. The blackness around us was replaced by a pale dawn sky. It was disorientating, and I blinked to clear my vision as we swooped down into the lush, green valley that lay beyond the portal.

Lucian flew up beside me, dipping his wing in greeting. We must have made a strange sight, flying in tandem with our unusual cargo. Beneath us, Stavrok's palace lay glittering in the early morning sunlight, its multitude of windows shining up at us.

Hopefully the king wouldn't stay long in the human world. He needed medical attention, and his wife would not be happy when she found out he'd stayed behind.

We flew toward our own home, the weather shifting into our winter wonderland.

By the time we flew over the mountain range that divided Damon's kingdom from Stavrok's, even the colder, thinner air couldn't dampen my spirits. I clutched the still-unconscious woman close to my chest, hoping the warmth of my dragon body was enough to protect her from the harsh elements of the north.

Up ahead, my half-brother's castle loomed on the horizon. I steeled myself and prepared for the descent.

There were people already standing on the castle battlements, waiting for us, as we flew homeward.

I circled overhead, eyeing Lucy, Marienne, and Erik's upturned faces. As Lucian and I landed on the rough flagstones, they rushed us from every direction.

"What happened?" Lucy asked, her forehead creased with worry. She kept looking up at the sky, until she must have figured out Stavrok wasn't with us.

She reached out to grab hold of the girl in my grasp and a faint ripple of anger swept through me, demanding that my mate stay close by my side, but I shoved it down. "Where's Stavrok?"

I let go of my dragon and shifted back, standing on two feet once more. Marienne rushed forward, handing Lucy a blanket for my mate, and a thick robe for me, which I took gratefully.

"He's heading back to your castle. He had some things to take care of first."

Lucy's gaze narrowed, before studying my faintly singed hair. Beside me, Lucian straightened. There was a purpling bruise on his cheekbone; he must have been hit by a piece of falling rubble when we'd been at the house.

"Dymitri," Lucy said, putting her hands on her hips. "What *happened?*"

I didn't have the energy to pretend. "Stavrok got shot."

The queen's hands flew up to cover her mouth, and I spoke quickly before she had a chance to interrupt. Or panic.

"He's fine. Injured, but alive. He said he'll get the palace doctors to attend to him, and he'll be waiting for you when you return."

"He better be," Lucy grumbled. "All right. I'll tell the servants to get the carriage ready."

On the ground a few feet away, Marienne wrapped my mate in a blanket. Lucian had the other human woman over his shoulder, and he and Erik were already striding toward the doors of a nearby tower.

I turned away from Lucy and hurried over to Marienne. I could barely take my eyes off my mate's pale, serene face. Her beautiful blonde hair spread out like a halo. My breath caught in my chest and I crouched down, unable to resist putting my hand against her neck to check her pulse.

Despite her unconscious state, it was still strong, thank goodness.

"Where are Damon and Cass?" I asked.

"They left for their honeymoon last night," Marienne murmured, watching me carefully. Despite her kindness toward us, I felt uneasy being alone with her. The sorceress's intense, violet eyes made me uncomfortable. It was like she could read my mind.

For all I know, she can.

"We need to get her inside. Warm her up properly." I grunted, hefting my mate's dead weight into my arms. Her fair hair spilled over my arms as I marched to the castle entrance.

Marienne fell into step beside me. Her apparent calmness was unsettling, considering my urgency. She held the door open for me and I swept through, letting her lead the way down the maze of passageways until finally we were at the door to an unfamiliar chamber.

"We had this wing of the castle prepared for the two women," Marienne said. "My vision showed me the state they would be in when they arrived. I knew they would need urgent care, and warmth."

Her brow furrowed as her eyes fell on the woman in my arms.

"Thank you," I said, sincerely grateful for everything she'd done.

Marienne nodded at me as I shouldered open the door, finding my brother already in the room. Erik and Lucy were nowhere to be seen.

The room was dark, softly lit by a few lamps set into the alcoves. Two beds had been placed side by side under a white canopy. On top of a cupboard opposite the beds, several medications were arranged in neat rows.

I ignored the anxiety that twanged in my chest at the sight of the make-shift hospital and made my way over to the empty bed. Gently, I deposited my mate onto it, and pulled the sheets up over her small body. Her skin was almost as pale as the bedsheets, and the deep shadows under her eyes were even more pronounced in the low light.

How can this delicate-looking woman be a dragon's mate?

I stared down at her unmoving face. I couldn't deny the possessive *want* that surged through my body every time I laid eyes on her.

Her proximity was satisfying on some bone-deep, primal level; I couldn't explain it, but I knew it was real. This was it. Somehow, impossibly, she was the one.

My hands skimmed over her shoulders as I tucked the sheets around her. She seemed tiny beneath my hands. Most of the women in this realm were sturdily built and as tough as the menfolk—especially in the north. They had to be to survive the harshness of life. But this woman was a slip of a thing. One wrong move, and she would melt away with the morning snow.

When I glanced up at Lucian, I saw that he was staring down at the other woman, frowning.

I held back a grin.

Typical Lucian. Even seeing his mate for the first time can't make the guy crack a smile.

I opened my mouth to say as much to my brother, but before I could, Marienne slipped silently into the room. I straightened up again, feeling like a kid caught with his hand in the cookie jar.

Marienne swept over to the beds and stood between the women. She reached out and put one hand on each of the women's temples, closing her eyes for a moment. When she opened them, she nodded to herself, before turning to us.

"These girls have been through hell," she said, her face grave. Her eyes sharpened, their purple hue darkening into midnight blue as she pointed a finger at me and then Lucian. "They aren't like us. You will have to win them over slowly. Even when they heal physically, their mental suffering has been great. I don't know how long it will take before—or *if*—they will trust again."

She stared down again at the girls, and the expression on her face shifted as she took in the face of the girl Lucian hovered over. She frowned, a small wrinkle appearing between her usually flaw-less brows.

My unease grew and a shiver ran over my skin. "What's wrong?"

Marienne's eyes snapped up to meet mine.

"I... Nothing." She bit her lip, glancing at the woman again. "I'm just confused, is all. I saw two sisters, but this one—she wasn't in my vision."

I stared down at the sleeping, peaceful face. The resemblance between the women was clear: long, fair hair, pale skin. The one Lucian had brought back looked a little younger than my mate; perhaps still in her late teens.

"What are you trying to say?" Lucian demanded.

"I'm sure it's nothing." Marienne's hasty tone didn't match the nervousness in her eyes. "My visions are... sometimes a little unreliable. Perhaps I misinterpreted something."

I found myself nodding. The feelings swirling inside me were so real, so intense... I knew who my mate was, and if the sorceress had seen two sisters in her vision, then there was no doubt this young woman must be the one for Lucian.

When they wake up, that's when everything will start to make sense.

At least, I hoped so.

Too soon, Erik and Marienne took to the battlements to begin their long journey home. I watched with a heavy heart as the sorceress climbed onto the back of her mate. Even though she unnerved me, it was tough that our only source of guidance was leaving.

I wanted Marienne to be here when the girls woke up, but I knew this was something my brother and I had to experience for ourselves. Erik lifted into the sky, but before his powerful wings carried them away, Marienne twisted around and shouted down to us.

"Don't forget what I said!" Her voice traveled through the

whistling air as her flowing hair twisted in the wind. "Take your time with them. Please."

I nodded to let her know I'd heard, and then Erik's huge, leathery wings soared into the distance. Soon enough, they were nothing but a speck on the horizon.

I headed back inside the castle thrumming with nerves and anger. Who had done this to our mates? And what level of suffering had they endured, that Marienne was so nervous about their ability to heal?

Would we ever get the revenge my dragon already demanded for their suffering?

THREE

DYMITRI

The court physician was an elderly man who peered at us through half-rimmed spectacles as we ushered him inside the chamber.

"I've never treated human women before," he said, before reaching out to pick up my mate's limp arm. As he took her pulse, a throb of possessive rage rushed through me. I shoved it down. The physician was only trying to help them.

"But the basic principles are the same as for our kind," he continued. "They are dehydrated and exhausted, chafed from being in restraints, but I can't find anything else physically wrong with them at the moment. Not without speaking to them and doing a more thorough exam. When they wake up, they will both need bed rest, and lots of fluids."

I nodded my thanks and the physician soon took his leave. Like most of the staff in the castle, he was uneasy around my brother and me, not speaking unless necessary and slow to meet my eye.

Many people here thought King Damon had been a fool to let

the likes of *us* into the royal court. The courtiers saw us as thieves and scoundrels, trying to drag the land to ruin.

I could only hope that, over time, we would manage to change their minds. But it didn't really matter to me whether or not we achieved that. If we had to leave the castle and return to our rougher lives, I would do it. I had learned the hard way through life, that Lucian was the only person I could truly count on; we were used to living in a hostile world.

Though now, I had a mate I had to consider. I wasn't yet sure how that might change things, for my future.

I took a jug off the top of the dresser and filled the empty glass at her bedside with water. I hated being so powerless, but there was nothing to do except wait for my mate and her sister to wake up.

"Dymitri."

My brother's voice dragged me out of my thoughts. "Yeah?"

"Those feelings everyone describes getting when you first see your mate..." He didn't meet my eyes. "Do you feel them?"

I thought about the intense pull in the pit of my stomach. The desire that raged through me. My shifter burned with passion for this stranger who lay unconscious between us.

"I do." I swallowed, clenching my fists and then releasing them.

"What's it like?" he whispered.

I frowned, taking a closer look at Lucian. He was staring down at the other woman, focused intently on her face, like he was willing her to wake up. A ripple of confusion shot through me.

"What do you mean, what's it like?" I tilted my head, trying to get a read on him. "Don't you *feel* it?"

Lucian hesitated, then shook his head. "I... don't feel anything. She's pretty, I suppose... but there's no *attraction*. I rescued her because she was in trouble... but I would have done the same for anyone in that situation."

I thought back to what Marienne had said. Her confusion over her vision.

Maybe she's made a mistake...

No, surely it wasn't possible. It *couldn't* be. I wanted my brother to have *everything*. The fierce joy that burned through me dampened at the possibility that he didn't share in my passion for his mate.

"When she wakes up," I found myself saying, "Your shifter's bond will likely activate then. That must be the difference—my mate was awake when we found them."

"Maybe." Lucian didn't seem convinced, but I was.

Surely Fate wouldn't be so cruel as to deliver me my mate, and at the same time deny Lucian the mate he'd always craved?

Sarah

I woke up warm, beneath a deep, soft cloud. At least that was what it felt like as I slowly pulled myself out of the depths of sleep. I was almost drowning under the comfortable weight. I could sleep forever cocooned in its delicious warmth, and my body certainly wanted to.

But something at the back of my mind prodded me to *wake up*. There was something I was meant to do... something I'd forgotten.

I opened my eyes a fraction and my fingers closed around the cloudy substance which turned out to be a thick, plush blanket.

Wait. A *blanket?*

My eyes slowly adjusted to the dim light and I took in the room. It was lit with candles and had stone walls like a medieval castle.

This must be a dream...

My heart hammered inside my chest. Was I in a hospital?

It didn't feel like one. There were no nurses, no blinking lights.

It didn't smell like a hospital ward, either; instead of antiseptic, the air was scented with woodsmoke. The scent was divine, permeating my nostrils and causing me to inhale deeply.

What is that beautiful scent? Who does it belong to?

We'd been saved! That was certain.

Thank God for that. Our nightmare might finally be over.

My eyes opened a little wider. In the corner of my field of vision, I made out a fireplace full of bright, flickering flames.

What the...?

My breathing picked up as panic set in. I wanted to speak, but when I opened my mouth, nothing came out.

Nadia! Nadia, where are you?

Through my half-closed eyelids, a dark shape appeared. A cool glass was pressed to my lips, and I swallowed rapidly.

The sensation of water passing through my parched lips was pure bliss and I collapsed back on the pillow with a sigh, my eyes closing even though I tried to keep them open.

Where am I? And who are you? I wanted to ask my water bringer, but the dark shape receded out of view. I was too weak to open my eyes again, or even lift a finger.

I slipped away into darkness once more.

THE NEXT TIME I WOKE, daylight cast brightly over my face.

This time my eyes flew open easily.

There was a thick canopy, woven with strange patterns, above my head. It stretched right over the bed and draped down on either side, then tied at the bases of the ornately carved pillars.

I squinted in confusion. *Why am I in a four-poster bed?*

I shifted experimentally, pressing down. My fingers met a soft, downy mattress. I rolled my head to one side, feeling the lush pile of pillows beneath me.

Is this some kind of hotel?

My heart squeezed with elation. Had we been rescued? I must have passed out because I couldn't remember how we got here. The memories leading up to this moment were a dark blur as well.

I had a faint memory of the delicious smell of woodsmoke, and the sound of our captors shouting in panic.

And then... I must have dreamed the next part. It was... impossible.

Nadia!

I sat bolt upright with a gasp, instantly taking in the room around me. There were stone walls, huge, arched windows, a roaring fireplace—and my sister's small frame, half-buried in blankets, asleep in the bed across from mine.

Oh, thank God!

I scrambled to push my sheets away and stumbled to my feet, my heart thumping wildly in my chest. I took a step forward, and the world tilted. My fingers grasped for the bedside table, but before they could make contact, something warm and solid collided with my back, and strong fingers wrapped around my hand.

"Whoa!" The deep voice came from behind me and it made the hair on the back of my neck stand on end. "Easy, little one."

I wanted to tell him I wasn't a horse, and despite my size I wasn't helpless, and he didn't need to treat me that way. But my knees were wobbling, practically knocking together like a new-born foal.

I tried to move forward, but the stranger held me back. "You must rest, woman. You're too weak to move about just yet."

I struggled against him. "My sister! She's—"

"She's fine, but weak. She's still recovering from her ordeal." The voice was firm, which was oddly reassuring. "As are you."

I stopped fighting him and allowed myself to be led back to my own bed. The world was spinning again.

Damn it. I hated being so weak.

As I settled back down onto the pillows, I got a good look at the owner of the deep voice. My heart leapt with a mixture of fear and fascination as I met his eyes for the first time.

I know those eyes...

"You," I blurted out. "You're the one who broke into the basement. You're the one who... who..." *He saved us.*

I fumbled, lost for words. Fragments of memory slipped through the fingers of my consciousness. I remembered clawed talons, and dark, scaly skin... the shadow of wings against a blackened sky...

And most vivid of all, fire. Blazing bright and hot, destroying everything in its path. Reducing the house that had been our prison into a pile of smoldering ash.

Large hands wrapped around my wrists, and I realized I was clutching the bedsheets in my fists.

"You're safe here," he said. "I promise."

I twisted away from his touch. "Where am I? What is this place?"

The room was like something out of a painting. My gaze landed on the plush rug in front of the fire, on the crossed swords and shield that hung above the fireplace. I wanted answers, but everywhere I looked only increased my confusion.

"Somewhere you can rest," the man said. "Trust me. You are safe."

I couldn't escape those piercing eyes. They were such a light blue they bordered on gray. The color reminded me of a frozen river. They were still and guarded at their surface level, but a storm of emotion raged beneath. I wasn't sure how I knew that, but in my heart, it was the truth.

The intensity of his gaze made my breath catch in my chest.

He appeared to mistake my flushed cheeks for something else, because he pressed the back of his hand against my forehead.

"Are you feverish?"

I shook my head. Some instinct made me draw the bedsheets up over my arms, cocooning myself from his touch. I craved his touch, which was the exact opposite of what I wanted or needed at this time. It made my evasion of him, even more necessary.

"Where am I?" I forced myself to meet his gaze. Even though my pulse was racing, I tried not to let the fear show on my face.

He didn't look like any of the men who had kept my sister and me captive. Truth be told, he didn't look like any man I'd ever met in my life.

His dark, shaggy hair curled around his ears, and the dark stubble on his face made me question just how long he'd been keeping watch over me. A scar cut through the stubble on one side of his face, running down to the edge of his jaw. His bare forearms were weathered, and more scars crisscrossed the tanned skin there, faint, pale lines that intersected, some old, some new. He looked like a warrior of old, but that was insane. Nothing in my experience had prepared me for someone like this guy.

He watched me calmly. "You are in my brother's castle."

My mouth dropped open. Did he just say… *castle?*

My fingers didn't budge from their death grip on the sheets. I couldn't help but feel like a cornered animal on high alert. A glance downwards confirmed that I was still wearing my clothes, at least, but it was cold comfort.

"Okay," I snapped, terror and annoyance warring within me. "How did I get to this… *castle?*"

"I brought you here."

Simple as that. My stomach twisted at his words.

"And you'll let me go once my sister wakes up?" I persisted. "We're not prisoners here, are we?"

As we had been back at the farm.

He shook his head. "No, of course you're not a prisoner. You're only here to recover from your injuries."

I relaxed a little, though I noticed he hadn't totally answered my question.

"My name is Dymitri," he said, when the silence stretched out between us. "I still don't know yours."

Despite everything, I almost smiled. He had brought my sister and me to this unknown castle, surrounded by who-knew-what, totally at his mercy. But he didn't know my name. And clearly, he wanted to.

"Sarah," I managed eventually. To my relief, my voice didn't tremble, and I managed to keep my head held high. "My name is Sarah."

I'd never thought my name was anything but plain. But from the way Dymitri's eyes suddenly darkened, and my belly did an answering flip-flop, my name suddenly seemed like the most erotic word in the world.

FOUR

DYMITRI

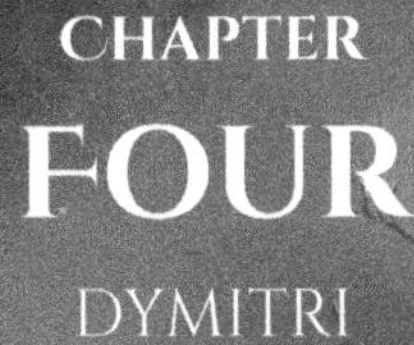

I held my breath as I walked to the bedroom door to let myself out. I had to force my dragon down with every step I took.

When I reached the door, I turned the handle, then glanced back at her. "I will return shortly."

I waited on the threshold, eyeing her until she nodded. She was still looking at me warily, but she was no longer half-buried in the blankets, which I took to be a good sign.

The sight of her threadbare clothes reminded me that she needed something new to wear. Food, too. Who knew when she last ate?

I headed into the corridor, only to find Lucian hovering just outside the room.

"How are they?" he asked, barely giving me time to shut the door.

"The one I rescued—Sarah—she's woken up." I fought to keep my voice even. I wanted to shift, to fly far above the clouds. I could have burned the whole place down with my desire for her. But I had to keep myself in check for now. "The other one is still out cold."

I caught the attention of a passing servant and waved him over. "Some bread and hot soup, please. For two people. Quick as you can."

The man gave me a smile which looked more like a sneer, turned on his heel, and strode down the hallway. My hands clenched into fists. I knew very well what most of the servants saw when they looked at me: a bastard son of the old king.

Rejected. Unwanted. Desperate.

The reminder always stung, though King Damon made sure we never felt it in his presence. Cass and Damon treated us like family.

"I'll go to the kitchens," Lucian said. "Just to make sure the cooks know we need food up here."

I nodded as he followed the manservant out of sight. I listened to the echo of their footsteps until silence fell once more.

I was abruptly aware that I was alone... and Sarah was waiting for me on the other side of the door. My heart hammered in my chest as I pushed it open and peeked in.

Maybe she's gone back to sleep.

I swallowed hard at the sight of the empty bed. The bedcovers were rumpled, and Sarah was gone.

My blood ran cold. I stepped into the room, ready to bellow out for help, and woe betide anyone who didn't respond.

Then I saw a small figure, sitting beneath the window.

Sarah turned her head as I moved to stand beside her. She was curled up on the narrow window seat, feet tucked underneath her, staring with seeming calm out at the frozen landscape beyond.

"I thought you were gone." I tried to keep the note of accusation out of my voice.

I wouldn't have blamed her if she'd tried to escape; after everything she'd been through, it would have made sense.

"I just wanted to stretch my legs. And see it for myself." She turned back to the window, pointing at the snow that drifted past the glass. "I guess you were telling the truth about this being a castle."

I hesitated before dropping down onto the other end of the seat, shifting awkwardly to accommodate my large frame. She still seemed calm enough, but from the way her eyes kept darting toward me, I could tell she was on edge.

"I would never mislead you." I kept my reply soft and as non-threatening as possible. "This is an ancient fortress. It's been in my father's family for generations."

Her bright blue eyes widened as they met mine. Her lips hovered apart, like she was on the verge of questioning me further. I was transfixed by the soft bow-shape of her mouth.

God, she's perfect.

Then the door opened, and Sarah's mouth snapped shut. Her gaze dropped down to her lap, and I frowned as she shrunk into herself, shoulders hunching.

Lucian approached with a tray and set it down on a nearby table. I smiled when, despite her obvious anxiety, Sarah leaned forward. I inhaled the scent of the fragrant soup and hot bread that my brother had brought and my stomach tightened in hunger.

"Please, eat." I gestured toward the tray.

When her eyes narrowed, I shrugged, reaching for a hunk of bread and tearing off a piece.

"Suit yourself," I said, dipping the bread into one of the mugs of soup and then shoving the food into my mouth. I grinned at her.

Her mouth curled into a nervous smile. She reached out, took her mug from the table, then took a few careful sips of soup before hunger seemed to get the better of her and she grabbed for the bread and began eating in earnest. Before long, she had demolished half the tray.

By the time she was finished, her eyes were brighter, and her skin had lost that deathly pallor.

"You must have been hungry." Lucian raised an eyebrow at her.

Sarah's hands were still curled protectively around the mug, but she nodded. The movement made her fair hair shift around her shoulders and catch in a momentary ray of sunlight. I wanted to reach out, to run my fingers through the strands of her hair... I struggled to focus back in on the conversation.

"I haven't had a meal like that in..." She trailed off, fingers tapping against the mug. "I don't know how long."

"Those men," I growled, and her eyes snapped up to meet mine. "Who were they?"

Her cheeks paled so much I almost regretted my question. Lucian frowned at me, and I knew what he was thinking. She was too weak right now; any unnecessary stress might impede her recovery.

I needed to find out what those bastards did to her and her sister and punish them for it, but I wanted to see her get better first. That was the only thing standing in the way of me going back through the portal right now and killing every last one of them.

At first, I thought my anger had scared her into silence. But after a moment, she started to speak. Her voice was quiet and hesitant at first, but the more she spoke, the stronger she seemed to become.

"I was... well, I *am*... in my final year of college. My little sister Nadia had come up for the weekend, just for a visit." Sarah's eyes darted to her sister's still-motionless form. "She'd always been the one of us to stay at home. She went to a community college close by, so she could look after our parents. I was the one who wanted excitement, the adventure of the city… Anyway, on the last night of her stay, I wanted to go out. She didn't want to… but I insisted."

Sarah's voice wobbled and her eyes shone with unshed tears. I wanted to reach out and pull her close, but I resisted, giving her the space to continue in her own time.

"Anyway, we eventually went out. After hitting a few clubs, I wanted to try this new place, on the edge of town. She went along with it… but I knew she wanted to go home. The street was dark, and we'd been walking for…God knows how long. Anyway, at some point a man stepped out of the shadows. Before I could do anything, something hit me in the back of the head… and I woke up in the back of a van, with Nadia by my side."

"What did the men want with you?" Lucian asked.

My hands were clenched together in my lap and I breathed shallowly through my nose. Sarah wiped a stray tear from her cheek.

"They told us they'd kidnapped dozens of girls—girls like us —from all over the place. Some of them ended up working for their business." She sniffed.

My mind flashed back to the women gathered around the table in that dimly lit room, handling the drugs.

"But they said we were too valuable for that. A pretty face could fetch a high price. They'd have buyers lined up for both of us soon enough."

Sarah's voice trembled and she collapsed as she burst into tears. The stress of everything had apparently caught up with her. I put my arm around her shoulders, wanting to offer comfort. At first she stiffened up, then relaxed into my touch.

My heart ached with happiness to hold her, and my dragon was calm knowing his mate was here, and safe at last.

When she spoke again, her voice was barely above a whisper.

"I don't know long they kept us in there. At first, we were held in one of the back rooms... and Nadia thought we could escape. She waited until she thought everyone was asleep, and tried to slip out." Sarah closed her eyes and shuddered. "When they brought her back, the man in charge got angry. He—he hit her, hard, and she fell. She didn't get back up. After that, they put us both down in the basement in those chains."

I pulled her closer, feeling her ragged breathing against my chest. "I'm sorry you had to go through all that. Rest assured, no harm will come to you here."

She pulled back from me and wiped her hands over her face. "I just want to go home."

I exchanged a glance with Lucian. Minutely, he shook his head at me.

He's right. I need to be careful what I say. don't want to shock her any more than I already have.

Instead of answering her directly, I decided to change the subject. "Now that you're awake, I'll see about getting you some clothes." I plucked at her threadbare sleeve. "You must be half frozen."

"Why are you doing all this, Dymitri?" Her eyes met mine, sharp and suspicious. "How did you know where to find us in the first place? Why are we here?"

Whatever I'd expected from this human woman, I could see that things weren't going to be as straightforward as her recognizing me as her mate and simply falling into my arms with joy.

I reluctantly pulled myself away from her and stood up. "Excuse us for a few moments. I'm going to see about some garments for you."

Once Lucian and I were out in the hallway, he rounded on me, arms crossed.

"You can only stall for so long," he said, as we fell into step. "Sooner or later, you're going to have to tell her the truth."

"I know."

She was beginning to trust me; I could see that. But how long could I keep her in the dark about our bond? About her new life in this land? Would she change her mind and want to stay? Or would she still want to go 'home'—to the human world?

Our connection was so new and still so fragile.

I stole a glance through a window as we passed, eyeing the stormy sky with trepidation.

How long before it all came crashing down?

Sarah

I DON'T KNOW how long I sat at the window, watching the snow falling over the frozen landscape.

From what I could see from my high vantage point, the castle was expansive. Below us, stone gargoyles scowled from ornately carved cornices, and the spikes of various towers rose into the sky.

There were snow-covered hedges in the gardens below, and the occasional staff member hurried along the steps that snaked down toward a heavy iron drawbridge.

It was like a castle from a fairy tale, or a dream. I kept expecting to wake up in the cold basement. But the longer I sat there, the more I realized that this was real. We had been rescued, and now Nadia and I could begin the road to recovery.

I pressed my fingertips against the leaded glass window, watching my breath fog up the surface. I shivered, reminded of Dymitri's promise to find me something to wear. It was warm enough in this room, with the fire roaring in the grate, but some warmer clothing would be welcome.

Right on cue, a soft tap sounded on the door.

"Come in!" I called out.

I was expecting Dymitri, or his solemn-faced brother, but instead a petite woman entered the room. Her arms were piled high with fabric. I was up out of my seat in an instant.

"Don't trouble yourself, ma'am." She ushered me down again, before dumping the pile onto my bed and giving me a once-over, her hands on her hips. "By the looks of you, picking this lot up would finish you off, so to speak."

She paused, biting her lip. "Sorry to speak out of turn."

She didn't look that sorry, but I didn't care. I was just relieved to have some friendly conversation to interrupt my whirling thoughts.

I shook my head at her. "You're probably right. What have you got there, anyway?"

"New clothes for you, ma'am." Her sharp gaze flickered over me, lingering on my face and hands. I tucked them into my lap, suddenly self-conscious. When was the last time I'd had a bath? As if she'd read my thoughts, the woman said, "Perhaps I can show you the facilities first?"

"That would be great." I clambered up, relieved at the prospect. Earlier, I'd been half-starved, and too traumatized to think of such things. But now...

The maid opened the door at the far end of the room.

There was a bathroom in here? Amazing!

She held the door open so I rushed over and slipped across the threshold. My mouth dropped in wonder.

Instead of cold gray stone, the room was covered from floor to ceiling in a warm, honey-colored marble. In the center, a giant sunken bathtub dominated the space. I craned my neck to admire the cascade of multi-colored light filtering through the stained-glass skylight above our heads.

"Wow." I couldn't help but laugh a little with amazement.

How the hell had I ended up here? Maybe I'd died in that rotten basement, and this was my version of heaven? Food, warmth, incredible bathroom facilities... and a huge hulking man who generated strange feelings deep inside me, especially when he looked at me with more desire than I was used to.

"There are towels and robes in that cupboard." The maid pointed to a huge armoire in the corner. "Will that be all for now, ma'am?"

"I guess." I gave her an awkward shrug. "Uh, there's no need to call me ma'am. Please, I'm Sarah."

"Of course." The maid gave me a smile. "I'll be just outside."

Once I was alone, I turned my attention to the giant bathtub. The prospect of soaking in a mountain of bubbles had never been more tempting.

After a frustrating fight with the taps, I managed to fill the tub with hot water. The plumbing was unlike anything I'd ever seen. But then, I hadn't exactly visited a castle before.

A quick search in the cabinet across from the sink yielded a wide assortment of jars and bottles, full of all kinds of scented products. Some of them smelled familiar and reassuring—lavender, rose, violet—but some of them I couldn't place at all.

I sank into the hot, fragrant water with a moan. Whatever my reasons for being here, I might as well enjoy the opportunity to have a good wash.

I soaked until I began to get impatient to be really clean. So, I grabbed some of the soaps and washed every inch of my body, then finger-combed my hair and scrubbed it the best I could. My hair was matted and disgusting until now, and once I was done, my arms ached from exhaustion.

It was all so strange. This castle. The wild weather outside. My confusion over how exactly we had been rescued...

But the strangest thing of all, by far, was the man who'd been watching over me when I awoke.

Dymitri.

For some reason, my mind kept turning back to him. I couldn't get his face out of my mind, or the intensity in his ice-blue eyes whenever he stared at me. Which was basically all the time.

I shivered as a gust of cold air grazed over my bare, wet shoulders. I stood up quickly and wrapped myself in a soft towel from a nearby pile. My heart rate had picked up again, and my toes curled against the marble floor when I remembered Dymitri's fierce expression. The expression belied the gentle warmth of his hands as they wrapped around my wrists, holding me steady.

No harm will come to you here.

My mouth twisted into a soft smile. I didn't know why, but when he said it like that... I'd actually believed him.

But what of Nadia? Was she safe here, too? And what would happen to her when she finally awoke?

She was the most important thing to me, and I owed her so much. It was my fault we were in this whole mess, and I had to make sure I never forgot that fact.

I opened the door and stepped back into the warm bedroom. "Sorry, I didn't catch your name."

The maid looked up as I re-entered the room, wrapped in a fluffy robe. I was loose-limbed and warmed through after my bath, and I smiled when I saw she had laid out some garments for me over the bed.

"It's Isla, ma'am—I mean, Sarah."

"Isla." I padded toward her, sparing a glance at the other bed. "My sister... did she wake at all while I was gone?"

My heart sank when Isla shook her head.

"No. I kept an eye on her, but she didn't stir. She seems peaceful enough," the maid added, clearly catching my look of dismay. "And the physician came earlier and checked you both over. He said you will both need food and drink and rest, but that, physically, you will be all right."

Physically? What about mentally? Oh Nadia. What have I done to you, dear sister?

I leaned over Nadia's bedside and put my hand to her forehead. Her face remained perfectly still. Only the soft rise and fall of her chest under the bedsheets reassured me that she was still alive.

With a deep sigh, I brushed the hair back off her face, and then turned to Isla.

I plastered a cheery smile on my face. "So, what do people wear to keep warm around here?"

The answer to that question, apparently, was way more complicated than I expected.

Isla handed me stockings, silk dresses, jackets made from soft wool, fur trimmed hats and coats, lace-up boots, and a multitude of other items until the room looked like a hurricane had swept through it. A lot of the stuff was familiar, but some wasn't.

There were boots made out of something tougher and thicker than leather, and a gauzy dress that reminded me of dragonfly wings, but somehow it was warm and seemed sturdy.

"Where did all this stuff come from?" I struck a pose in a floor-length fur coat that was much too big for me, making Isla laugh. "Did you raid a mall or something?"

A puzzled expression crossed Isla's face. "Some of it belongs to Queen Cassandra. The rest used to belong to the king's mother, rest her soul."

My skin prickled with discomfort. These clothes belonged to royalty. I'd never heard of a Queen Cassandra, but still...

"Are you sure it's okay for me to borrow them?" I laid the coat over the back of a nearby chair, smoothing it nervously.

"Of course." The confusion on Isla's face grew. "Why wouldn't it be?"

Before I could give her an answer, the door opened, and that put an end to our conversation.

Dymitri was back.

∼

Dymitri

Now that Sarah was in the castle, it was torture to stay away from her.

Lucian and I had been sparring in the yard in an attempt to keep my passion in check. It worked well enough; that familiar burst of adrenaline that came from a good fight managed to distract me from the constant itch under my skin.

But once the sun began to dip lower in the sky, I didn't have the strength to avoid her any longer.

After I took a shower, my feet carried me back to the door of her room. I hesitated before entering.

Her scent hit me as soon as I crossed the threshold. I fought to keep my expression neutral, but the shifter inside me rumbled in satisfaction at the mere sight of her.

She met my eyes with a nervous expression. The maid had decked her out in clothing from our realm; she wore a simple fur trimmed dress with a neckline that skimmed just below her collarbones.

She looked exquisite. The very sight of her made me want to push her down onto the bed behind us and take her right there and then. Claim her as my own.

I managed to meet her eyes, hopefully without telegraphing my lascivious thoughts, and she gave me a small smile. I returned it, clenching my hands into fists so that I wouldn't do anything stupid.

"What do you think?" She gave a small twirl, holding her hands out expectantly.

"Better," I bit out, my dragon desperate to take over my human body. I shoved it back down. "C'mon, let me show you around."

Sarah's gaze strayed toward her sister's bed. "Maybe I should stay..."

"Don't worry," Isla said from the other side of the room. "I'll stay here with her, and take care of her if she wakes. We'll get her some food and a bath, like you had."

"Thank you, Isla." Sarah smiled at the woman, before following me toward the door.

Once we were out in the hallway, I glanced down at her, surprised by how quickly she seemed to have found her footing around here. That didn't seem to extend to me, however; every time we locked eyes, her cheeks reddened.

Not that I was doing much better. My shifter stirred restlessly; every time our hands brushed, or I caught a waft of her delicious scent, the dragon inside me leapt up, ready and eager.

At the end of the corridor, Lucian appeared. When he saw the two of us together, his eyes narrowed as if with suspicion. He could tell how close my dragon was to the surface.

"I am just going to give Sarah a tour of the castle." I raised my eyebrows at my brother, trying to project an innocent aura. "And the village."

"While I'm here, I might as well see it," Sarah added. "I've never been inside a castle before."

My chest twinged with unease. I didn't want to lie to my mate, but I didn't see much of an alternative. It was better this way; too much too soon might cause her to completely shut down on me.

Lucian caught my eye. I could feel his disapproval, but he said nothing.

After we had turned the corner, Sarah looked up to me with a questioning expression. "Your brother seems... quiet."

My mouth twisted into a smile. "Yeah, always has been."

"I don't think he likes me very much."

"Don't take it personally." I moved to touch her arm, before thinking better of it. "He's like that with everyone."

"You're not. You're different." Sarah's gaze burned into the side of my face.

I stared blankly at the tapestry in front of us, trying to quiet the shifter inside me.

Control yourself.

As I led her around the castle, the quiet, frightened woman I'd met disappeared; her eyes were brighter, and the way she held herself became more confident. With her long blonde hair and regal clothes, she looked every inch a dragon princess.

She paused in front of a giant portrait in the hall. It towered over us, looming from above.

The old king stared down at me with foreboding, judgmental eyes. Beside him, his queen sat with a serene expression, with baby Damon on her knee.

"Who is *that?*" Sarah whispered.

I took a long pause before answering her. "That's my father."

Her eyes widened. I could see the wheels turning in her head, trying to connect the dots.

"Does that mean..." She pointed at Damon. "Is that you?"

I let out a humorless laugh. "No, that's not me. That's the current king, Damon. C'mon, this way."

We wandered over to the doors that led into the main hall, Sarah eyeing me curiously the whole time. I pretended not to notice her regard.

I didn't want to talk about my father. Not now. Not ever, in truth.

Sarah lingered in front of the huge stained-glass window that dominated the front of the hall. The glimmering, colored panes told the story of the winter kings. How they had come to this land, hundreds of years ago, and built the castle where we now stood.

"See those mountains?" I pointed to the images in the bottom of the stained-glass window, and Sarah nodded. "Those lie to the south. Damon's ancestors journeyed over them so they could build this kingdom here in the north."

Sarah's upturned face was filled with wonder. The colors of

the window shimmered over her skin and tangled in her long hair.

A spike of desire pierced through my soul.

I looked away, choking on the maelstrom of feelings that surfaced for the human before me.

"And those creatures?" Sarah indicated the top of the window, where several large dragons circled overhead. Their glassy wings shone in a multitude of colors: deep reds, vibrant greens, and pale blues that scattered light over the floor down by our feet. "I've never seen anything like *that* in a window this old."

I gazed up at the dragons, my heart sinking.

I can't keep lying to her forever.

But for now, I had to settle for a half-truth. "You could say that they're an important emblem in the royal family."

Sarah's eyebrows rose, and I could tell that she was on the precipice of another question.

"This way," I interjected, ushering her over to the door. "I want to show you the village."

Sarah

SOMETHING WASN'T ADDING UP.

With every hour that passed, I felt stronger. My mind got clearer, and the world around me became real again. How long had I spent in a dreamlike stupor, just trying to make it from one day to the next, while my sister and I had been imprisoned?

But now, I had food in my belly and warm clothes on my back.

I could *think* again.

And every instinct was telling me to hold my cards close to my chest.

I glanced over at the man walking beside me. I couldn't

understand why, but when he was around, I felt... better. Calmer, safer.

Even though I was in a strange place, surrounded by strange people. He had shown me great kindness, even if he occasionally seemed unsettled by me.

From the way he mentioned his father, I sensed that there was a lot more to the story.

I shivered as a blast of cold air hit my face. Dymitri grinned at me.

"Now you know why all our clothing has a fur lining." He laughed, holding the front door to the castle open for me.

I descended the uneven stone steps carefully. My shoes had a good grip to them, but a thin layer of ice beneath my feet made the going difficult. I almost took a tumble, but at the last second, he grabbed my elbow.

"You should watch where you're going." Dymitri's deep voice murmured in my ear. "I might not always be around to catch you, Sarah."

I am not blushing. It's the cold air biting my cheeks, that's all.

"Easy for you to say," I retorted. Dymitri moved with an enviable confidence and ease, taking my weight against his shoulder like it was nothing.

Which, given his size, it probably *was.*

Dymitri laughed, and my stomach flipped over at the sound. "I've navigated harsher terrain than this, believe me."

Once we crossed over the narrow wooden drawbridge and hit the cobblestones, I could breathe easier.

We were in a tiny village and, as we made our way down the narrow, crooked street, I took in all the sights and sounds. Overhead, the sky was a pale gray, and white flakes were still lightly spiraling onto our heads.

Where in heaven's name are we?

"Welcome to the village." Dymitri's voice rose above the

hubbub. "This is where the castle gets its supplies. People from the outlying farms come to trade, to pay tithes, that kind of thing."

"Wow." I paused beside an old woman selling bundles of fragrant herbs, before glancing up at Dymitri. "Tithes? That sounds pretty old-fashioned."

Like... medieval.

"I suppose it would," Dymitri said with a shrug. His pale eyes scanned our surroundings, like he was half-expecting someone to attack us at any moment.

A dozen follow-up questions sprung to my lips, but before I could voice any of them, I got distracted by another seller: a cheerful, red-cheeked man selling sweet, candied apples in the next stall. They smelled mouth-wateringly delicious.

Dymitri followed my gaze. "Do you want one?"

"Oh..." I bit my lip. "No, it's okay."

"One toffee apple," Dymitri said firmly to the man. "Thank you."

"Right away, Sire." The apple seller skewered one of the apples for me and handed it over. When Dymitri dug around in his pockets for the cash, the man waved him off. "No charge. Your royal custom is payment enough, my prince."

"Nonsense." Dymitri pulled out a handful of coins and shoved them into the bewildered seller's hand. "I always pay my debts. I'm no *prince*."

"My deepest apologies..." The seller seemed uncertain which form of address to use and trailed off.

To spare him any more embarrassment, I gave him our thanks and dragged Dymitri further down the street.

Dymitri's eyebrows had drawn down, but I kept my hand on his arm hoping to distract him a little. When I took a bite of the apple, his eyes tracked the movement of my mouth. For some reason I liked that he did that, and I deliberately licked my lips, chasing the sugar at the edges of my mouth.

God, what is happening?

"So, let me get this straight." I took another bite of the apple, smiling at the explosion of sweetness over my tongue. *So good.* "Your father was the king, but you're *not* a prince?"

"It doesn't work like that." Dymitri hesitated, eyes searching my face. I waited. "I wasn't born here in the castle. My father was king... but my mother wasn't the queen."

Oh.

"I'm sorry." I stared down at the red glazing on my apple, my cheeks burning. "I didn't mean to pry."

"It's nothing." Dymitri's finger nudged against the side of my chin. Gently, he tilted my face upwards, then brushed a strand of my hair away from my lips. "That's better."

I stood there, transfixed by the look on his face. No man had ever looked at me the way Dymitri did... especially not one that I'd only just met.

Despite the fact that I barely knew him, I couldn't deny my racing heart. Nor could I explain the way my body leaned into his, like it wanted to close the space between us and hadn't consulted with my mind about its intentions.

Abruptly, Dymitri stepped away from me. His jaw was tight, a hard line against the dark fall of his hair.

"Let's continue." He forced the words out through gritted teeth, and turned his back on me entirely.

I had to run to catch up with him as we wound our way through the street.

I was certain the flush in my cheeks had spread to my neck. In fact, it felt like my whole body burned with heat beneath the thick winter layers of clothing.

When he finally slowed his pace, I took a deep breath and

exhaled. "So..." I adopted a casual, bright tone that rang hollow. "Where to next?"

We stopped at half a dozen more stalls. Every time I thought we were done, something new caught my eye: a stall hung with huge, dried mushrooms, a cart laden with different smoked cheeses, a black velvet tablecloth covered in smoky quartz. It was all so beautiful. And different to anything I had ever known in my life.

The dank basement and those terrifying rough men felt like a lifetime ago.

So long ago, in fact, it now seemed like a distant nightmare, and I'd finally awoken. The relief was enough to send me staggering.

Eventually, we reached the edge of the village. I frowned at the narrow dirt track that led out toward what looked like miles of bare, frozen wilderness.

I couldn't understand how such a thriving community could exist in the middle of nowhere. How had they even gotten here?

A shout pierced the air, and my attention shifted to a small group of men on the other side of the road. Three of them held a wooden frame, and after a second, I worked out what it was—the bones of a house.

One of the men yelled something to the others. The words got whipped away in the wind before I could understand them, but they caught Dymitri's attention. We watched as the man struggled; one of the support beams at the corner of the structure had shifted out of place.

"That thing will come crashing down if they're not careful," Dymitri muttered, seemingly to himself.

A creaking groan came from the frame. It was bending in the wind, twisting even more out of shape, threatening to snap altogether under the strain. A volley of shouts followed the noise. A small crowd gathered around the men but no one seemed willing or able to step in and help. It would take inhuman strength to hold the beam in place.

Dymitri and I glanced at each other. Without a word, he darted forward, ushering people aside. When the village folk near to us got a good look at him, they stepped aside, murmuring to each other, their eyes wide. Dymitri hardly seemed to notice. I hurried after him. Once we reached the center of the crowd, he stepped forward and grasped the errant beam with both hands.

"On my count," Dymitri shouted at the men on either side of him. "Lift!"

Despite a sea of dumbfounded looks, they did what Dymitri told them to do. Dymitri, seemingly stronger than the rest of the men put together, eased the frame into place with no difficulty.

Once the structure was secure, a scattered round of applause started up amongst the onlookers. The other men offered their thanks to Dymitri, who waved them away. He didn't seem comfortable with all the attention. In fact, the longer we stood there, the more he started to glower.

I was beginning to wonder if his seemingly natural propensity toward anger was actually a mask to hide his awkwardness with others.

An elderly woman stopped us as we headed away from the crowd. The deep wrinkles around her eyes grew as she smiled up at Dymitri. Her eyes shone. "Blessings to you, Sire."

Dymitri shifted uncomfortably, and I fought back a smile. I was right. He was uncomfortable—especially, it seemed, when people showed kindness toward him. He must have had a difficult life indeed, if he didn't feel worthy of receiving niceties from others.

I could see that he wanted to correct her address, but he didn't want to come off as disrespectful. Eventually, he settled for a half-nod, lowering his gaze.

"Thank you. And to you," he mumbled.

Once we were out of earshot from the gathering, I put my hand on his arm. He seemed startled by the sudden contact, but he didn't push me away.

Our footsteps echoed loudly across the cobblestones.

"You know..." I bit my lip, feeling a little bit cheeky. "I've never met royalty before, but you aren't what I expected."

Dymitri tilted his head down to look at me.

"I told you." His pale blue eyes were intent. My skin prickled under his scrutiny, but I didn't drop my gaze. "My brother and I aren't royals."

"But you're not one of the villagers, either. What you did back there... it was a true kindness. It also showed exceptional strength. You did a good thing, Dymitri."

His expression twisted, and he glanced away from me, rubbing a hand across the back of his neck. "I saw a problem and stepped in to fix it. Anyone would have done the same in my position."

Unconsciously, my hand had found its way back onto his arm. I squeezed gently to make him look at me again. "That's not true."

I didn't know if it was the softness in my voice, or the way I was holding on to him, but something shifted in his expression. He moved closer to me, and for a dizzying second, I wondered if he might actually lean in and kiss me.

I should have been scared and jumped back. But I wasn't, and I didn't. Instead, I waited, my heart beating strangely fast.

In the end, he stopped just short. His tone was grave when he finally spoke, and something in his eyes made my heart rate speed up even more.

"Sarah. There's..." He cleared his throat. "I have to show you something."

"Where are we going?"

I didn't know how many times I'd asked that question. It didn't matter—Dymitri gave me the same answer he had all the other times.

"You'll see."

It was maddening, and yet I had no choice but to follow him. If I turned around and left him now, I'd get lost for one thing. For another, I had to admit that he'd piqued my curiosity.

He led me all the way back to the castle, then through a network of hallways and corridors, until we reached new doors and went out into the gardens. I thought at first we were heading toward the massive hedge maze lying beyond the rose garden, but instead Dymitri drew me to a halt in the little courtyard at the bottom of the steps.

"Well?" I crossed my arms, waiting. "What is it?"

Dymitri looked... nervous. He took a few steps back from me, coming to halt about ten feet away.

"I need you to promise me something."

I shuffled from foot to foot, beginning to grow uneasy. "Okay."

Dymitri bowed his head. "Promise me you won't be afraid. I would never harm you. *Never*. Do you understand?"

I wanted to laugh out loud. After everything I'd just been through, he wanted me to trust he'd never hurt me? I wasn't sure I could promise that. I wasn't sure I would ever trust anyone fully again.

But something in his demeanor told me to take this seriously. After a moment I nodded, once, my fingers tightening protectively around my forearms.

"All right. I'll do my best." It was all I could offer.

He looked at me for a long moment. "Very well."

He crouched to the ground. My eyes narrowed, wondering what he was doing, then widened in disbelief as a thick mist filled the air around us. The cloud rose up, higher and higher, until it blocked out the sky.

I inhaled sharply as the impossible happened right before my eyes. The man before me disappeared. His limbs grew larger, his fingers turned into claws, and, most terrifying of all, a huge pair of wings, with curved spikes crowning each wingtip, rose up out of the swirling fog, like great, dark shadows.

The enormous monster before me threw back its head and let out a roar that shook the ground beneath my feet and rippled into the air.

"Holy shit."

He looks like... My blood froze with terror. *A dragon?*

I took a stumbling step backwards, then another, backing up until I was at the bottom of the stairs.

I couldn't think as the enormous creature advanced on me. In that moment, everything Dymitri had said vanished into the ether. I was nothing but prey for the monster that was stalking toward me.

My heart pounded like a war drum in my chest. The roar of my blood in my ears was so loud I couldn't hear anything else.

I wanted to run, to hide, but my feet were rooted to the ground. I could do nothing but watch as the mist began to clear, and the massive dragon stood before me, head lowered, staring at me expectantly.

Dymitri...?

My breath caught in my throat as my eyes climbed up over the creature's thick, scaly hide. The light glinted wickedly off its claws. In contrast with the pale landscape, the dragon was an inky black color, aside from its eyes...

Which were as piercing and intense as the man himself.

When I locked eyes with the dragon, something inside my chest eased. My fear began to drain away.

That gaze was so familiar. This creature—this *man*—wasn't going to hurt me. Deep down in my soul, I knew it.

I inched forward, reaching up into the air between us, my fingers outstretched.

There was nothing but silence around us, and the softness of the still falling snow. My own shallow, uneven breaths came out in little puffs of fog.

When my fingers made contact with the creature's chest, I inhaled with shock. I had expected ice-cold scales, but instead, my fingertips were met with a smoldering heat, like I'd touched glowing coals.

I jerked back, but then I realized the warmth wasn't burning me. It was *caressing my skin,* wrapping me up like a thick, soft blanket.

I put my hand to the dragon's scales and stroked down them, keeping my touch light and gentle.

The creature lowered its head, eyes sliding shut. It let out a deep rumble of satisfaction that resonated through my whole body.

This is impossible.

But I couldn't deny the evidence of my own eyes. I let out a breathless, slightly hysterical chuckle.

My roaming fingers encountered a deep gouge of old scar tissue. I frowned, moving to the side, peering closer to get a better look.

The dragon's thick shoulder was covered in a mass of scars, running all the way down from its neck. In a flash, I remembered the scar on Dymitri's jaw.

Who could have done this to such a beautiful, majestic creature?

I pressed my forehead against the scales, feeling the warmth emanating from within, comforting myself by listening to the slow, steady pulse of the dragon's heartbeat. A wave of sorrow for his suffering threatened to pull me under as tears rose in my eyes.

I sniffled, and let out a soft sob, squeezing my eyes shut. It was no use, though; a few salty tears leaked out and fell.

Under my hands, the scales fell away, and bare skin returned in its place.

"Shh." At the sound of Dymitri's deep, rumbling voice, my breathing slowly evened out, and I relaxed against him. When I opened my eyes, I realized that the warmth surrounding me was his embrace; strong arms, holding me steady on my feet. "It's all right. I told you, nothing will hurt you here."

"What happened to you?" I whispered.

"Many things."

I sniffed, wiping my face and drawing back enough to look him in the eye.

"In time, I'll tell you." He reached out and swept a strand of my hair back behind my ear. "I'll tell you everything, Sarah."

~

Dymitri

I'd controlled myself long enough for Sarah to drag her hands over my body. In my shifter form, I was even more volatile in relation to the mating call, but somehow I'd managed not to react to her touch in the way I truly wanted to.

It was only when her tears wet my skin that I couldn't hold back. The dragon retreated, and I was left standing before her. Just a man, standing in front of the woman he was meant to love.

I pressed my body against hers until she got a hold of herself. It broke my heart to see her like this, to feel how vulnerable she truly was.

I pressed my lips to her forehead as she looked up at me in wonder. There were still tears in her eyes, but awe as well.

"How..." She bit her lip, shaking her head. "How is this even *possible?*"

"For my people, it's normal." I swept an arm out around us, indicating the castle and the vast lands beyond it.

Her eyes brightened further in recognition. "Wait... so those dragons in the window..."

I nodded. "Almost everyone in this realm is a shifter." I stared down at my feet. "I happen to come from one of the royal bloodlines, that's all."

If I'm telling her everything, I might as well get it over with.

"This is insane," Sarah murmured. She glanced toward the horizon, shaking her head.

"Sarah." I reached up to grip her shoulders before I could stop myself. "Search your memories. How do you think we rescued you from that farmhouse, back in your world?"

She frowned. "Hang on... what do you mean, *my* world?"

"Come inside," I said. "Let's get warm. I'll explain everything, I promise."

Her gaze drifted downwards, and her cheeks flushed as she seemed to realize for the first time that I was completely naked. I watched with amusement as her gaze fluttered around, not knowing where to look.

Of course. Humans have hang-ups about such things.

"When we shift, our clothing shreds," I murmured.

"Oh. Err... okay..." She still couldn't look at me, and I had to bite my cheek to stop from laughing.

Once we were back inside, I found a thick robe and slipped it on. I caught Sarah sneaking glances more than once at my bare chest still exposed, but this only served to further heighten my excitement. It was becoming clearer than ever that our interest in each other was mutual.

Remember to take it slow. A voice that sounded suspiciously like Lucian's protested in the back of my mind. *This is all new for her.*

Once we were situated in front of the huge, roaring fireplace in the Great Hall, it was difficult to think about anything else. Sarah stared into the flickering flames, her skin bathed in golden light. Her long hair flowed down her back, brushing against her bare neck as she leaned into the warmth.

"So?" She arched a brow toward me.

My mind turned blank. I struggled to remember what we were talking about. All I could think about was how beautiful she looked in the flickering firelight.

Oh. Right. Worlds.

"Outside," Sara said patiently. "What did you mean, *my* world?"

"This place," I said, gesturing to the stone walls, the gargoyles peering down from the rafters, the snow that swirled outside the huge windows, "is not part of the human realm. It exists beyond a portal."

A small crease of confusion appeared between Sarah's

eyebrows. "Portals... dragons... those words tell me I'm dreaming. I must have been knocked on the head or something."

I smiled softly at her. "You're not dreaming. We found you and brought you here."

"Let's assume that what you're saying is true." She tucked her feet up under her. I mirrored her position, sitting cross-legged on the cushion opposite. "How did you know where to find me? It's not that I'm not grateful, but... why am I even here?"

This was it. The moment of truth.

I still wasn't sure she was ready, but her face was open and inviting, and the way she kept biting her full lower lip was driving me to distraction.

"Our kind... we're not like humans. In life, we're fated to end up with one partner. Some of us never find that one person, but when we're lucky enough... they stay with us forever."

Sarah tilted her head, puzzled. "Like... a soul mate?"

I didn't know how to describe something I barely understood myself, but I nodded.

"Yes. A soul mate. Two halves of the same whole, who are only complete when they find each other."

Reflecting the firelight, her eyes brightened as she mulled over my words. "What does this have to do with Nadia and me?"

"My brother and I... we have a friend. A sorceress. Her name is Marienne. It was her vision that led us to you."

Sarah's eyes widened. "A *sorceress?* Hang on, wait a second. Are you saying... do you think *I'm* this fated person?"

I nodded, my heart thundering. "Nadia is Lucian's fated mate. And you, Sarah, are mine."

The silence that followed my words lay between us. The unspoken tension that had been building since she woke up had finally reached a breaking point; from the look on her face, we were both feeling it.

"Is it really so hard to believe? Can you really tell me that since we met, you haven't felt anything?" I reached out to hold her wrist loosely in my hand. "I can feel your heart rate pick up when I touch your skin. I see the way your pupils widen when you look at me."

Sarah just stared at me, dumbfounded. "I..."

I slid my hand over hers, and her fingers automatically turned to slide over the bare skin at my wrist. "Even now, you can't deny yourself."

"This can't be happening," Sarah said in a small voice. "I barely know you."

But her hands had already moved of their own accord; one of them had come up to rest on my shoulder, and the other dipped down to my chest. The shifter inside me growled in satisfaction under her touch, and I smiled.

"You will," I whispered, just before I brought my mouth down to meet hers.

~

Sarah

DYMITRI'S KISS SURPRISED ME, but not for long. I couldn't stop myself from responding, tentatively at first by lifting my chin and returning his kiss, before eagerly grabbing hold of his hair to tug him closer.

I wasn't sure what had come over me. Perhaps I was still in shock from seeing him transform into a dragon and back. A *dragon*!

But I knew it was far deeper and more elemental than shock. I could not resist him, and I did not want to.

My enthusiasm only seemed to spur him on. His kiss began softly, with light, melting brushes against my lips. Then the connection shifted, deepening further and further. Eventually he groaned and tilted my head backwards, dragging his mouth down my neck and sucking hard at my pulse point.

My breath hitched in my throat as he grabbed my waist and tugged me closer.

I climbed on top of him and straddled his thick thighs, moaning as his big hands clamped around my hips and held me tight.

He plundered my mouth, and I wanted more. *Desperately.* I *needed* more. I slid my arms around his shoulders and then up to his neck, trying to give as good as I got.

I squeezed my arms tight, a slow, lazy warmth coiling in the pit of my stomach at the feel of his hard muscled form against my body. My reservations melted away, replaced by a haze of desire.

Dymitri arched up with a growl, rolling us over. I found myself pinned to the floor as he lavished open-mouthed kisses onto my neck and chest, dragging his teeth lower, over my racing heart.

I swallowed thickly. My arousal mingled with surprise. Then worry. This was all going so fast. He was on top of me, surrounding me, bending me to his will.

Our eyes met, and I fought back a gasp. His pupils were blown out, inky black with a thin sliver of ice blue around them. His mouth was red, and as he panted down at me, there was a flash of white teeth.

I squirmed, my hands grasping for purchase. He groaned and rolled his hips into mine. It felt good, but I couldn't push away my fear. He was so strong, and his passion threatened to drown me.

His hips bore down into me again. His hard length pressed down into my belly. It felt so good and so right, but my fear continued to grow. I shuddered, twisting, and he snarled at the sensation of me moving beneath him.

When his fingers slid up beneath my skirt, the fright consumed me. I urged us over, and he rolled onto his back, looking up at me. His chest heaved, robe-half open.

He was so damn sexy, but suddenly, I couldn't breathe.

What am I doing?

I scrambled off him and stumbled away. His hands shot out as if to draw me back, but I darted out of reach.

I have to get out of here.

He growled again, and for a split second, I thought his dragon was going to emerge. But when I caught a flash of his expression, I realized he was fighting to keep control of himself. To stay as Dymitri the man, and hold the dragon inside.

He stretched out his fingers toward me. "Sarah... Please..."

He sounded like a dying man, on the verge of his last breath. I ached to return to his arms, but my fear had taken hold and threatened to consume me.

"I'm sorry," I whispered in a broken tone, before I turned and ran.

I tore down the dark hallways, taking random turns until I was totally lost. Behind me, Dymitri's faint voice called for me, but I ignored him and kept running until I was certain I was out of his reach.

I came to a trembling halt beside a huge tapestry and slid down the stone wall opposite, collapsing into a heap on the floor and heaving in deep, ragged breaths.

I glared at the swirling patterns in front of me. Embroidered dragons flew through a woven landscape, strong and majestic. I dropped my gaze to my lap and hugged my knees in close.

I want to go home.

But I couldn't leave. Not while my sister was still lying unconscious in another part of the castle. I had to stay and ensure her safety.

Plus, there was a huge part of me that ached to return to that warm fireside. To be held in Dymitri's arms again, to listen to him tell me that everything was going to be okay. That I was safe.

What is wrong with me?

I rested my head on my knees and squeezed my eyes shut.

At the faint sound of footsteps coming from the other end of the corridor, I stiffened, on high alert. I tried to remain as still as possible, praying that the shadows would conceal me.

I'm not ready to talk to him. Not yet.

But the voice that called out to me wasn't Dymitri. It was a female.

"Hello?" The pattering footsteps grew closer. "Is anyone there?"

I sniffed and drew my legs in closer. "Please leave me alone."

My voice was trembling and thready in the echoey space. Instead of retreating, the stranger came right up to me, dropping into a crouch in front of me.

"Are you okay?"

Although I'd buried my head in my arms, I could almost make out a mass of curly dark hair, and a sweet, heart-shaped face. The voice was kind and gentle. Despite my fear, I looked up, meeting the eyes of the young woman.

"I'm fine," I lied, wiping a hand over my face. "I just got lost, that's all."

Instead of offering me a hand up, the girl shuffled onto the floor beside me, resting her back against the wall.

"This place is kind of a maze, huh?" She smiled at me, her cheeks dimpling. "Not to mention the *literal* hedge maze outside. Have you explored it yet?"

After a small pause, I shook my head.

"You should—it's great." She released a small sigh and stretched out her legs over the floor. "I'm Cass, by the way. What's your name?"

"Sarah."

"Nice to meet you, Sarah." Cass's cheerful voice made me relax a little. "What brings you to our castle?"

Other than a mythical beast? Not much.

Oh, my God. Didn't someone mention the king's wife was named...

Cassandra?

I took a closer look at her. The thick, fur-trimmed collar around her neck, the cuffs at the end of her sleeves... her outfit was almost identical to my own. She wasn't one of the servants who roamed the halls, which meant that...

"Your Majesty," I stammered. "I—I'm so sorry—"

"Hey, stop!" Cass put a hand on my arm before I could embarrass myself any further. "It's okay, Sarah. Don't worry! We just got back from our trip, that's all. You surprised me!"

"I didn't know where else to go," I said. "I just needed some space to clear my head."

"What happened?" Cass folded her arms under her chin, studying me carefully.

I let out a deep sigh. "Dymitri brought me here."

Her eyes widened as realization set in. "Oh, my... you're *her,* aren't you? The human woman that Marienne saw in her vision?"

Human woman? "I guess I am," I mumbled. "He told me that we're... fated to be together, or something. And then he... changed."

I didn't know how else to describe a guy turning into a huge dragon right in front of me, but Cass seemed to get the gist, nodding along. Hell, Dymitri told me that they were all like him. That probably meant she had the same power.

"So, what's the problem?" Cass prompted me softly. "Don't you like him?"

"It's not that." I struggled to get the words out; my thoughts still tangled together with my knee-jerk desire to *escape.* "He's amazing. Like no guy I've ever known, to be honest."

I let out a nervous chuckle, and Cass smiled encouragingly.

"But the way he *looks* at me... it's like there's something inside him, driving him to... take me. *Claim* me. It's so intense." I sighed. "I had to get out of there."

I looked up, fearful of her response.

But her expression was understanding. "You're a human, Sarah. This is all new for you."

"I don't want to hurt him." My voice trembled as the tears threatened. "I don't want to hurt anyone."

Especially someone who'd shown me nothing but kindness since I woke up.

"You haven't." Cass laid a hand on my arm. "Dymitri knows the score, Sarah. He'll understand. It's difficult for dragon shifters to resist the call to mate. He wouldn't have meant to scare you. I'm sure he was being as gentle as it was possible to be, in the circumstances."

I thought back to the ferocity with which he'd held me, the inhuman growl he'd let out as I'd run away. I shivered.

Cass seemed to sense my wariness. "Look—I don't claim to know much about the human world. I'd love to visit it one day, but... I know that things are different there. Dymitri would never harm you, Sarah. He'll let you take things at your own pace."

"How can you be sure?"

"Because I know him. And his brother," Cass replied. A soft smile played on her lips. "They captured me once—Dymitri and Lucian. I thought they were going to hurt me, but they gave me food, warmth, and shelter. They're loyal men, Sarah. Loyal to my husband, and to you and your sister."

"Your husband..." I remembered the painting of the royal family in the hall. "King Damon."

Cass nodded. "We just got back from our honeymoon. Things weren't easy with us, at first. I'm from the south, you see. We're from different worlds."

"I know the feeling." I shared a weak smile with her. But her kindness had calmed my anxiety somewhat. Slowly, I unfurled my legs and sat upright. "So, what's the deal with this bond? How does it work?"

"No one is sure." Cass shrugged. "Even the sorceress, Marienne. But all dragon shifters have a mate. Some just happen to be human. You probably have shifter ancestry in your bloodline, if you go back far enough."

I didn't know how to begin unpacking *that*. The thought that one of my grandparents, my great-grandparents, could be one of those creatures...

My alarm must have shown on my face because Cass chuckled. "Come on. Why don't we go down to the kitchens and get some hot chocolate? It's so draughty up here."

I clambered to my feet alongside her and shook my head. "Thanks for the offer, but I think I should go back and find Dymitri."

I had no idea what I wanted to say, but talking to Cass had cleared away some of my worries. I was going home anyway. My time here was limited only to the time it took for Nadia to wake up and become well enough to travel.

Maybe I could just take this one step at a time and see where the road led me—and the first step was to talk things through with my so-called "mate".

Cass smirked. "Okay. Go find him."

I turned to walk away, then chuckled. "I could use a hand getting back, if you don't mind?"

Cass laughed and slid her arm into mine. "Not at all."

Dymitri

I stood with my eyes closed under the jet of scalding water, inhaling the steam that rose around me. I pushed my wet hair back from my face before letting my hands drop to my sides again.

My fists clenched as another wave of regret swept through me.

I've screwed everything up. I've driven her away, forever.

Lust still churned inside me, and my shifter thrashed ceaselessly, furious at being ignored. But it was muted due to the pain. I'd made my mate run away, and I couldn't forgive myself for that.

I let out a deep sigh. She would want to leave now; I was sure of it. And it was no one's fault but my own.

I was in the middle of working out how I would explain myself to Cass and Damon when the door to the room outside opened and closed softly, and light footsteps followed.

They paused outside the bathroom door. Whoever was out there was listening to the shower, hesitating.

I imagined one of the servants there on the threshold, one hand on the doorknob.

I opened my mouth to tell them to leave. Whatever royal business it was could wait; I needed to clear my head and make preparations to take Sarah home.

The thought pierced like a knife through my heart.

If she won't stay with me, the least I can do is make sure she gets back to her family safely.

Before I could say anything, the door opened, and the person stepped into the bathroom. I watched their progress as they crossed the room. The shower cubicle was large, but the glass was too fogged up to see clearly who it was. I caught a blur of movement as they came closer.

My heart rate picked up. I recognized that small frame, the blonde hair, and that scent. Her beautiful, enticing scent.

Sarah stepped out of her garments, one after the other, leaving them on the floor where they lay. By the time she reached the glass door behind me, I was hard and wanting.

The door opened.

Sarah stood naked before me. My gaze raked over every inch of her creamy skin, devouring the vision she presented. Her pert breasts, her rosebud nipples, the graceful curve of her hipbones... all of it set me on fire.

My cock was already skyward. I couldn't remember ever wanting—no, *needing*—anyone as much as I wanted Sarah in this moment. I didn't know where I wanted to put my mouth first, but I stopped myself from moving, staying rooted to the spot as she joined me under the hot spray of water.

She looked up at me with wide eyes. She stood a hair's breadth away, close enough that I could feel the heat from her skin. Small droplets ran down from her hair, racing over her chest and stomach.

Still, I waited. "Are you sure?" I managed, though my voice was a mere croak. The last thing I wanted to do was scare her away again.

"Yes. Touch me," she whispered.

Those three words were all it took. With a groan, I took her face in my hands and kissed her, bringing her up on tiptoe and pressing her against my body. She was so soft, so willing.

I didn't know what had changed between earlier and now, but it wasn't the moment to stop and ask. From the way she was nibbling my bottom lip it was clear that she wanted me now. And that was enough for me, and my shifter.

We stumbled over to the tiled wall, and my hands slid under her wet thighs. I urged her upwards, wordlessly encouraging her to wrap her legs around my waist. She gasped, clinging to me like a lifeline. Her lips brushed my neck, and I shuddered, driving forward with her until she was pressed up against the damp tiles, spread out for me.

I lifted her higher and set my lips to her breasts, suckling her nipple deep into my mouth. First one perfect rose tip, then the other.

Sarah writhed against the wall, clinging to my head and filling the shower stall with her gasps.

I held her with one arm and moved my other hand to tease her flesh. I flicked my thumb over her clit, again and again, until she was crying out against me. Then, and only then, did I slowly slide one finger up into her tight pussy.

I groaned as she wrapped around my finger, her walls slick and ready for me. I added a second finger to stretch her some more. She wriggled and groaned as I thrust inside of her, listening to her gasps as a guide to what she wanted.

When she tightened around my finger, and her gasps became too loud to hold back anymore, I withdrew my fingers and grabbed her thighs with both hands.

With her arms looped around my shoulders, it was easy for me to slide into her. She was slick even under the force of the shower, and I groaned as I sank into her depths. *Perfection.*

Her heels drummed into the small of my back, and I began to thrust into her tight pussy, listening to her cry out in pleasure and allowing the sounds to drive my own desire higher.

"Please," she whined, pressing her face into my shoulder. "Dymitri... *please.*"

I groaned at the sound of her pleading, and continued to drive into her over and over, unrelenting with the need to claim her as mine. She weighed practically nothing, and it was easy to slide a hand free to get between our bodies and circle her clit with my fingers.

She squirmed with the extra teasing and her channel walls clamped tight on my cock. We were both wound up from earlier, and it wasn't long before the desperation in her voice told me she was about to climax.

I dropped my head to her neck, growling into the damp skin, sensing her fluttering pulse under my tongue. When I nipped at the skin, she cried out and began to buck in my arms as I felt her cum around me.

My shifter growled in satisfaction, and I tumbled over the edge after her, filling her with my seed and bonding us together at last.

EIGHT

SARAH

I woke up in a sea of soft sheets, a deep blue canopy above my head.

Blinking the sleep out of my eyes, I sat up, confused. This bed was massive, much bigger than the one in the room my sister still slept in…

My eyes landed on the man standing opposite the bed. He was staring out the window, lost in thought. My eyes lingered on the broad line of his shoulders, and my stomach curled with satisfaction as I remembered the night before.

My limbs dragged under the weight of the heavy blankets, soft and sated with the multiple orgasms Dymitri had given me last night. I stretched my arms above my head, taking a second to luxuriate.

"Good morning." Dymitri's deep voice provoked a smile across my face. "Did you sleep well?"

I nodded shyly, pulling back the sheets and hopping out of bed. I was still naked from last night's activities, but I found a robe lying over the back of a nearby chair and slipped it on before joining him at the window.

"I want you to join me today." Dymitri slid his arm around my waist, and I leaned into his warmth. "Damon and Cass are back from their honeymoon. They're waiting for us down in the Great Hall."

"I actually bumped into Cass yesterday," I admitted, my face heating. At Dymitri's questioning look, I shook my head. "Doesn't matter. Sure, that sounds great."

We headed downstairs together, pausing to check on Nadia. She was exactly the way I'd left her yesterday. The maid, Isla, was there watching over her.

"Any change?" I brushed my fingers over Nadia's forehead and squeezed her hand briefly.

"It's hard to tell," Isla said with a small frown. "Her heartbeat seems stronger today. But only time will tell when she wakes up."

"Thank you for looking after her," I murmured, a wave of guilt crashing over me. I hadn't been here watching her. Isla had. I'd been enjoying myself, making love to Dymitri while my sister lay here unconscious.

"Of course." Isla bobbed a curtsey to me as we left the room.

Dymitri pressed a kiss against the top of my head.

"She's in good hands," he murmured. His gaze slid back toward the room as we wandered further down the corridor. "Strange. I expected to find my brother in there."

I looked up at him, confused. "What do you mean?"

Dymitri shrugged. "If you were the one in that bed, I wouldn't have left your side. I'd be in there night and day until you woke."

A flood of warmth filled my chest.

"I guess he doesn't know her. She's just a stranger to him… and it's not like she's not well looked after."

A small crease appeared between Dymitri's brows. "I suppose."

I stood on tiptoe so I could kiss the frown off his face. "Come on. I'm hungry."

As soon as we stepped into the Great Hall, I gasped. A fire roared in the fireplace and a huge oak dining table was laden with all kinds of delicious-smelling food.

Dymitri laughed at the amazed look on my face. "It's something, isn't it?"

My eyes skimmed over the plates heaped with bread, the trays of sweet pastries, the huge silver coffee pot.

"I…"

It was like something out of a movie… or a long-forgotten dream. It was amazing.

At the head of a nearby table, Cass stood up and waved to me, her fork clattering onto her plate in obvious excitement.

"Sarah!"

King Damon himself stood up more slowly, subdued and regal in his movements. He nodded toward me and Dymitri. "Good to see you again, brother."

I glanced at Dymitri, not sure what to do.

Do I bow? Curtsey? Oh, God…

Before I could worry myself further, Dymitri strode forward and grasped Damon's hand, pulling him into a loose hug. When he stepped back, he was grinning. "How was the honeymoon?"

Damon's face relaxed into a smile. "A little warmer than I'm used to."

"We saw the coral reefs!" Cass interjected, sending a dimpled grin her husband's way. "It was *amazing*."

She turned to me, grabbing my arm and tugging me over to sit beside her. "I wish we could build a diving pool here, but it's way too cold. We might as well build an ice rink."

She picked up a piece of fruit, nibbling on it thoughtfully.

"We have the hot springs, love." Damon poured her a cup of something red from a nearby jug. The look they shared as he handed it to her was full of love.

"Hot springs?" I raised an eyebrow at Dymitri.

"The castle is built on top of a system of them," he said, passing me the plate of pastries. "I'll show you later. But right now, please eat."

I took a bite of pastry, closing my eyes in pleasure. It was heaven to eat proper food again, after all this time.

The door opened at the other end of the hall and Lucian appeared, looking as downcast as he had when I saw him previously. Dymitri hurried over to speak to his brother. They stood in front of the fireplace exchanging words in low, hushed voices.

Cass nudged my shoulder, and I tore my gaze away from the scene.

"Are they always like that—so private?" I asked the queen.

"Pretty much." Cass took a bite out of a roll and chewed thoughtfully. "They only had each other to depend on for years. And old habits die hard, I guess."

A deep frown appeared on Dymitri's face. Whatever Lucian was saying, it looked like Dymitri didn't want to hear it.

Seeing the two of them like that, silhouetted against the fireplace, it occurred to me once again just how different Dymitri was to me. He and his brother were so alike: tall and strong, with striking pale eyes. As the firelight flickered across the planes of their faces, they looked... formidable. *Inhuman.*

Which I guessed, was the actual truth.

Soon after their discussion ended, Lucian left the hall without even speaking to the rest of us. Dymitri returned to the table and his unsmiling face filled me with unease. His apprehensive expression was a far cry from the warmth and intimacy we'd shared this morning.

"Isn't Lucian joining us?" Cass leaned forward, sounding concerned.

Dymitri shook his head. "He's going for a walk. He needs some... space."

Damon and Cass exchanged worried glances. I couldn't help

but feel out of the loop, but the sensation faded away when Dymitri put his hand on mine, drawing my attention.

"Come on." He pushed a strand of hair behind my ear and tilted my chin upwards with his fingertips. "Let's finish eating, then I'll show you around the gardens."

THE NEXT FEW days followed a strange, but increasingly familiar pattern.

I would wake up with the sunlight hitting my face every morning, cocooned by Dymitri's warmth and solid arms. After an hour or so of mind-blowing sexual pleasure, we usually wandered downstairs to eat breakfast with the others.

I always checked on Nadia on the way to the breakfast room, and while she seemed to have a better color and was breathing more easily now, she still had not woken. The physician assured me my sister was mending, and would wake when she was ready. He had added a tube to her arm, via which she was receiving valuable hydration, and she seemed to be cared for very well.

At breakfast, Dymitri and I would chat with Cass and Damon, and I would ask as many questions as I could. They were helping me to understand the way things operated within the castle and this kingdom, and I found everything about the wintry palace fascinating.

Through the three of them, I learned something of the history between the brothers and their father... but only fragments. Whenever I tried to question Dymitri further on the king, he would often clam up, or drag me toward some distraction or other.

The castle itself was huge and rambling, with hundreds of abandoned rooms. Dymitri often went out on scouting trips with

Damon or his brother. Their dragons kept an eye out for enemies that might be crossing the vastness to attack us.

When they did that, I would check in on Nadia, and then Cass and I busied ourselves with exploring the castle.

According to Cass, a couple of years ago, the castle had been, in her words, "a total wreck". Things were changing now that Damon had taken the throne. But there was still a ton of renovation work to be done, not only here at the castle, but right throughout the kingdom. But before the rest of the healing could happen, all the junk from centuries past had to be organized.

That was where we came in.

One day, Cass and I were in a small tower room that felt like it hadn't seen daylight for years. She was standing on top of a small pile of broken furniture and old boxes, digging around like a determined hamster.

"Ah, ha!" She stood upright and grinned at me. "Victory!"

I peered at the object she'd unearthed. "A cradle? *That's* what we've been searching for this whole time?"

"I *knew* I'd seen it somewhere." Cass hopped down from the pile and began to tug on a box almost half her size, trying to shift it over. "It doesn't look like anyone's used it for years."

With a sigh, I moved forward to help her. "What do you need a cradle for?"

"You know," Cass said evasively. "Just in case."

I stared at her, puzzled. Then it dawned on me. She was newly married, and from what I knew about dragon mates, they were insatiable in the bedroom. My own experience with Dymitri had already taught me that.

"Are you pregnant? Not that you look it, of course..." My cheeks heated, and Cass burst out laughing.

"No! But it's never a bad idea to look to the future, right?"

"I guess." I still felt confused as to why she'd been so determined to find the cradle, but I figured it was best to go along with her.

Cass tugged the carved wooden cradle free from a tangle of old curtains, wiped away the dust on her hands, and turned to me.

"Sarah, are you happy?"

I looked up at her, startled. "Under the circumstances… surprisingly, yes." I bit my lip, fiddling with the cuff of my sleeve. "Other than my sister's condition, of course. I know she's healing, but I do wish she'd wake up."

Sometimes, I caught myself feeling terrified, right in the middle of a moment of pure bliss. It was a horrible feeling, but my worry for Nadia cast a shadow over the surreal happiness I'd found here. Until she woke up and I saw for myself that she really was going to be okay, I'd never be truly at peace.

Cass seemed satisfied with my answer. We climbed down from the tower to move on to other rooms, and I put the conversation out of my mind.

Until a couple of days later, when Dymitri and I were enjoying the hot springs, and he asked a similar question.

"Do you like it here?" His voice came out of the silence, echoing along the damp cave walls.

I was floating in the beautifully warm water with closed eyes when he spoke. I opened my eyes and lowered my feet to the floor of the pool, lazily regarding him. Condensation dripped all around us, and the steam rising from the surface of the water obscured his expression. I moved closer through the water and took one of his hands loosely in mine beneath the surface.

"Of course." I leaned backwards, floating on my back and staring up at the arched ceiling above us. "Everyone keeps asking me that. What's not to like?"

Dymitri was silent for a long moment. I reach out and brushed my fingers over his chest, tracing loose patterns across his firm shoulders. By now I knew every scar, every burn. Some of them I'd heard stories about, but the origin of other scars was still a mystery to me.

"The weather?" he said with a smile, trailing his fingertips along my collarbones. We were both naked, and the sensation made me shiver despite the lightness of his touch.

"I don't know." I slid through the water, and his hand dropped lower, cupping my breasts and thumbing my nipples with his broad, calloused fingers. I arched against him encouragingly. "It's growing on me."

His face broke into a grin, and he dipped his head to kiss me. I returned the kiss eagerly, groaning when he caught my bottom lip between his teeth.

When he pulled back, I whined, wanting more. But his eyes had turned serious. He held me at arm's length, just gazing deep into my eyes. My heart started to patter.

"What is it?"

Dymitri's hands slid up to cup my face, his touch achingly gentle. "Sarah... I want you to stay here."

My heart fluttered and a wash of confusion swept over me. "I'm already staying here. Until Nadia wakes up, right?"

I thought I'd been clear about that?

He huffed. "I mean, I want you to stay here with *me*, Sarah. Forever. You're my mate. I don't want us to be apart."

My shock must have shown on my face because he slid his fingers under my chin, forcing me to meet his eye. "You said it yourself—you're happy here. And for the first time in my life, I feel..." He closed his eyes and drew a deep breath before opening them again. "I feel at peace. There's nothing I want more than to share my life with you."

Was it my imagination, or did the water temperature suddenly drop several degrees? It felt as if the previous tranquility of the moment shattered; the steam around us pressed against my skin, and a jolt of claustrophobia made me reel back from his touch.

"Sarah." Dymitri's eyes darkened with confusion. "Surely you can't be surprised by this. You're my mate—it's natural I should want you here. I *need* you."

But I was already backing away, swimming over to the edge of the pool and climbing out of the water. I grabbed blindly for the nearest towel and began drying myself. My hands trembled.

"Come on." The tension in Dymitri's voice made me flinch. "At least let's talk about this!"

"I have to check on my sister," I informed him, pulling my overshirt down and drawing the laces on my boots. "She needs me."

"Sarah!" The water lapped over the edge of the pool as Dymitri swam across. "You're being unreasonable."

Anger burned in my chest. "*I'm* being unreasonable? You're the one who wants me to leave *everything* behind—my family, my home, my own *world*—to live in a place I don't even know! I'm not part of this world, Dymitri! I never will be!"

He opened his mouth as if to speak, those pale eyes gleaming like shards of ice. But instead of replying as I expected him to, with more placating tones to try and persuade me to stay, he gritted his teeth and growled at me. "Go, then!"

"Fine!"

I stormed over to the exit and blundered out of the cave, tears blurring my vision. I thought Dymitri might follow me, but he didn't, so I made my way back to the castle alone. By the time I arrived at the oak doors, a light fall of snow dusted the tops of my boots. I stamped them clean and hurried toward the main staircase.

He's crazy. I'm crazy! I got so caught up with him I forgot why I'm still here in the first place!

After all, didn't I have a family and a whole life waiting for me back home?

By the time I made it to Nadia's room, my anger had cooled down significantly. I was beginning to feel the first pangs of regret. Dymitri was a wonderful person and I knew that I'd never find anyone else who made me feel the way he did.

I need to talk to him.

That could wait, however. First, I needed to check on my sister because everything hinged on her and her health. Once she awoke, I knew that she'd be desperate to get home. To our family, our friends. Our lives.

And I'd have to go with her, because, just like I'd said to Dymitri, I didn't belong here in this world. Going home, to my own world, and my own life, was the right thing to do.

It was strange how that thought didn't feel *right* at all.

I waited in the pool until I was certain Sarah had gone.

My head thundered with pain, and regret pushed through me with the strength and heat of dragon fire. I'd been so sure that she felt the same way I did, but the look on her face when I'd asked her to stay here told me otherwise.

How could I have gotten it so wrong?

With a deep sigh, I heaved up to sit on the stone ledge. I glared down at my darkened reflection in the water as another wave of guilt crashed over me.

Ever since Damon had asked Lucian and I to stay in the castle with him, I'd been waiting for the other shoe to drop. For final confirmation, once and for all, that everyone would realize I didn't belong here. That I wasn't *worth* saving from the life I'd once barely survived.

I hadn't expected trouble to come in the form of a small human woman. She'd turned my world upside down in a few short days, and my life would never be the same.

My father's face swam up to the surface in my memories, just as foreboding and distant as he looked in that royal portrait in the castle.

"You're no son of mine." His remembered words reverberated through my brain. *"You are nothing."*

And now, my mate had rejected me, too. I was nothing to anyone.

Even Lucian had grown distant recently. At first, I'd attributed it to his worry over his mate, but whatever it was seemed to run deeper than that. He had always been taciturn, but now his continued silence had started to weigh heavily on me. Whatever it was, he had cut me off, which left me powerless to help him.

I had no place in the castle. Not anymore.

I swirled the water, breaking my reflection into pieces. Perhaps it was time to give up this life for good. I could head back out into the wilds. I'd survived there my whole life, after all. The life of a nomad was a lonely one—little more than hunting, ice-fishing, and basic survival. But at least I wouldn't hurt anyone else.

Everyone I loved, I hurt.

I jerked upright, my chest tight with a sudden realization.

I *loved* Sarah. With everything I had. This wasn't just passion and desire. This was *love*.

She was my mate, and I'd ruined things with her when they'd barely even begun.

And now I sitting here wallowing in self-pity, thinking about giving up on that love.

No. I was stronger than that. Better. And she deserved more than that from me.

As terrifying as it was to face the thought of more rejection, I knew I couldn't give up on Sarah. On us. Not at the first obstacle thrown in our path.

I scrambled up, disregarding the slick, damp stone underfoot as I raced to get dressed.

If she was truly my mate, then I would never give up on her.

I BURST through the castle doors and almost barreled into Lucian, who steadied me with both hands.

"Dymitri! What's wrong?"

I gaped at him, unsure where to begin. I felt like I'd just solved the world's greatest puzzle… and he was looking at me like I'd lost my mind.

"Nothing," I said, shrugging him off. "I'm fine. Just looking for Sarah."

Lucian arched an eyebrow. "Funnily enough, she just sent me down here to find *you*. Is everything okay between you two?"

My stomach twisted.

"I don't know," I admitted. "Wait, she's trying to find me? Why?"

Lucian's face was so pale and still, it may as well have been carved from stone. "Nadia's waking up."

My heart jumped at what that might mean. Without another word, I followed him toward the huge staircase. For once, I didn't pause to glance at the royal portrait that hung above the stairwell landing. Still, I could feel our father's eyes burning into the back of my head with every step.

I jogged to catch up with Lucian's retreating back. "Your mate is finally waking up. That's a good thing, right?"

Lucian glanced at me with a blank expression. "Of course."

His tone didn't fill me with confidence. The distance between us yawned like a vast expanse.

He nudged my shoulder. "What's the matter with Sarah?"

Quickly, I told him about our argument. How she wanted to return to the human realm and considered her time here nothing but a brief, forced holiday.

I fought to keep the misery out of my voice, but from the look on my brother's face, I could tell he wasn't buying it.

"Give her time," he said.

"She's a human and we're not." I sighed. "I understand her reservations, kind of. But I don't know if I can just... let her go. Now that I've found her, I can't imagine ever going back to the way things were before."

Lucian frowned. "Maybe that's the problem. She needs to talk to someone in her position, someone who's been through this before. You should take her south, to meet Queen Lucy. A human woman who became a dragon queen." He nudged me again. "She's bound to give her some good advice, from a perspective that we simply don't have."

I mulled his suggestion over in my mind. It wasn't actually a bad idea. I had to fight against my natural instinct to solve the problem on my own, but this wasn't about my ego, after all. It was about what was best for Sarah.

I hadn't met a happier couple than Lucy and Stavrok. I'd heard of their family, too: three healthy babies for the royal bloodline.

I suppressed a wave of envy.

I'd never given much thought to having a family. Up until recently, my life had been an unpredictable gauntlet of chaos and danger, hardly a fit environment in which to bring up a child. I'd lived the life of a warrior. Things like tenderness and beauty were distant dreams; they belonged to other lives, not mine.

Until the day I met Sarah.

"Maybe," I said with a grunt, eventually.

To my relief, Lucian didn't press me further. We reached the door to Nadia's room, and he paused.

"Hey." I put my hand on his shoulder. "You've got this."

I waited until he gave me a nod before I pushed open the door.

Sarah

I sat at the edge of Nadia's bed, holding my breath. Beside me, Isla hovered, folding blankets and fluffing the pillows on my old bed. The silence stretched out as we both watched the face of the sleeping woman.

Nadia sighed and frowned a little in her sleep. She drew a small breath, and her eyes opened softly.

"There," Isla whispered. "And just like that, she's back with us."

I couldn't contain the smile that broke across my face. "Hey, sleeping beauty."

My sister waking up was the most beautiful thing I'd ever seen, even with dark shadows under her eyes and hair that hadn't been washed in weeks.

Tears gathered in my eyes.

"Sarah..." Nadia mumbled, then lifted her head a little. A puzzled frown scrunched her forehead. "What happened? Where am I?"

Her expression was so familiar my heart clenched in my chest. I flung my arms around her neck, pressing my damp face into her hair.

"It's a long story." I sobbed. "I'm so glad you're okay."

Gently, Nadia extracted herself from my hug and blinked. "How long was I out?"

"Okay, don't freak out." I took her hand gently in both of mine. "Just over a week."

Not counting the time we were trapped under that house.

Nadia's face turned ashen. I picked up a glass of water from the bedside table and helped her take a shaky sip.

"Sarah..." she said, once I put down the glass. "Where *are* we?"

I glanced up at Isla. She gave a small shrug, looking just as lost as I felt.

How the hell do I explain this situation? I can barely wrap my head around it myself.

Luckily for me, a distraction arrived when the door opened and Lucian and Dymitri slipped through into the room.

My eyes locked onto Dymitri. A hundred emotions raced through me when I met those familiar ice-blue eyes. Guilt, regret, and confusion were the strongest ones of all.

"Sarah?" Nadia said in a small voice. She swung her legs off the side of the mattress and sat up slowly, gripping my arm for support. "Who are they?"

Right. The drama between Dymitri and me could wait. There were far more pressing matters to hand.

Like the fact that Lucian's mate had woken up, and he was confronting her for the first time. Would it be instant, like it had been for Dymitri and me?

Dymitri took another step into the room, shutting the door behind them. Lucian remained where he was, rooted to the spot. His face looked like a thunderstorm was brewing within him.

Dymitri glanced over his shoulder. "Brother, she's awake. Aren't you going to talk to her?"

Lucian still didn't move. He stared intently at Nadia. With every second that passed, the chill in the air grew stronger and stronger until it threatened to drown everything out.

"Lucian," Dymitri urged his brother again, then he glanced at me.

I was unsettled by the worry in his expression. Something was wrong.

I moved closer to Nadia, half-shielding her with my body. "What's wrong with him?"

"I don't know." Dymitri moved toward his brother and put a hand on his arm.

Lucian shook him off. His fists clenched tight. Even from my position beside the bed, I could see his white, strained knuckles.

"Lucian," Dymitri said, "you need to control yourself."

Lucian's lips pulled back into an unmistakable snarl, one I had only seen on Dymitri when he was about to change form. *Oh no.* I shrank back, pressing Nadia against the bed.

My sister wriggled out from around me and stood up, her hands on her hips. "Can someone *please* tell me what's going on?"

That was the last straw for Lucian, it seemed. The air thickened with dark fog, and a deafening roar reverberated off the stone walls around us.

"Sarah!" Dymitri shouted. *"Run!"*

A huge shadow loomed out of the mist. Lucian was in dragon form, his wings outstretched toward the high ceiling. One talon caught the candelabra above us and sent it swinging, before it crashed to the floor with a mighty boom.

I jumped as a burst of icy fire shot into the air. Nadia screamed.

I was afraid, too, but beyond the fear, fury rose. *How dare he threaten my sister? She's supposed to be his mate!*

My heart pounded in my chest at the realization that Lucian had gone insane.

Bloody hell.

"Stay behind me!" I yelled at Nadia, as the dragon circled around the edge of the room.

Before it could reach us, Dymitri dived in front of Nadia's bed to shield us from the monster.

I wanted to reach for him, but forced my arms back, trying to protect my terrified sister. "It's going to be okay," I gasped to her, not knowing if I believed the words.

Dymitri shifted right in front of us. Nadia cried out again, digging her nails into my arms, but I couldn't look away from him. He was magnificent.

Dymitri spread out his wings and snarled at his brother.

Lucian barely paused at the sound, continuing to advance towards Nadia and me.

Oncethe mist cleared, I could see his eyes, narrow pale slits above sharp teeth. His scales were paler than his brother's, more of a dark gray. Icy flames rose up and burst out of his mouth, burning cold and dangerous. If Dymitri didn't do something to stop him, there would be nothing left of Nadia and me.

I turned to my sister and wrapped my arms around her, pulling her close. "Close your eyes. Hold on to me."

With a rumbling roar, Dymitri launched himself at Lucian. From behind, me, I heard the sounds of them fighting.

My breath caught in my throat, fear pulsing through my blood. Not just for myself and my sister, but for Dymitri. He was fighting his only family, his brother. The man everyone had said was his best friend. His closest ally.

He was fighting his brother... to protect Nadia and me.

The room was huge and high-ceilinged, but even the castle's strong architecture was no match for dragon wrath. Wings caught against wall hangings, claws tore into curtains, and tables and chairs were upended as they fought savagely.

I screamed and jumped out of reach, pulling my sister with me as a chair clattered against my leg. I hurried her over to the wall, pressing her into the stones and covering her with my body as best as I could.

Lucian released a jet of icy flames that blasted a nearby wardrobe; Nadia screamed and I forced her out of its path just in time to feel the icy chill whizz over our heads.

Dymitri snarled in my direction, and for a second, our eyes met.

Get out! he seemed to be screaming at me. *Take your sister and run!*

But I couldn't move. I couldn't leave him, useless as I was in this situation. If I left him alone in this fight, he might not walk out of it alive.

Lucian seemed to be savage with rage, tearing into everything in his path. I could feel the pain and heartbreak radiating off him, and I knew Dymitri would only be able to hold him off for so long. That much pain... he was inconsolable that Nadia was not his mate.

Nadia's hand squeezed tight around my arm.

"Sarah!" she screamed into my ear. "We need to leave! Right now. Hurry!"

My feet were rooted to the floor. I was torn; my brain told me I needed to take my sister and go, but my heart said something else.

Nadia grabbed my arm and half-dragged me over to the door. She threw it open and yanked us both into the corridor, slamming the door shut behind us.

"I have to go back in there." The words spilled out of my mouth before I could stop them, and my sister's eyes widened.

"Go back?" she hissed. "Are you *crazy*?"

"It's Dymitri." I twisted in her grasp, trying to break free, but she held me firm. "I *have* to make sure. I need him to be okay!"

More crashing and howling issued from inside that room, and I had no idea what was happening.

Was Dymitri hurt? What could I do to help him?

Tears of frustration filled my eyes and spilled down my cheeks.

"Dymitri?" Nadia repeated. "You *know* one of those—those *things*?" Her eyebrows crept to the top of her forehead. "No. You're not going back in there. We're getting out of here, Sarah. We're lucky we weren't killed already!"

Her eyes flickered across my face. There was a desperation in her expression that was new.

My heart sank. This was my baby sister. It didn't matter what I wanted, what I *needed*; I had to make sure that she was safe.

And if I went back into that room, I couldn't guarantee that she would be.

Another screaming roar echoed from inside the bedchamber, and we both flinched back from the door.

"All right," I said, admitting defeat. A small part of my heart broke, as I added, "Let's go."

CHAPTER
TEN

SARAH

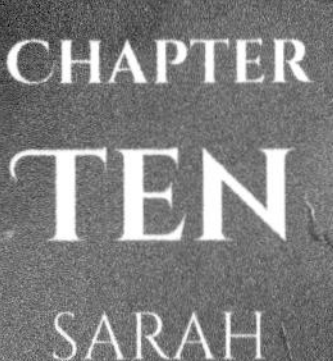

Nadia tugged me further and further away from Dymitri, my heart aching in my chest with every step.

"Come on, come on! We've gotta go!" she cried, dragging me down the main staircase and toward the front door.

It was only when we reached the bottom of the grand staircase that Nadia stumbled to a halt.

She stared up at the huge windows and elaborate stonework. "Whoa. What is this place?"

Our footsteps echoed loudly as we crossed the marble floor. I glanced down and realized that my sister was barefoot, and only wearing the long nightgown that the maids had dressed her in.

Damn it. She's going to freeze to death in this place.

I pulled off my jacket and wrapped it around her shoulders.

"A castle," I whispered. "Far away from home. Trust me, I'll explain everything."

Nadia shivered and pulled my jacket tighter around her. "Explain? You don't need to explain anything! We need to find a car and get home!"

Nadia's voice reached a squealing pitch and I reached out to grab her hand. "Please, calm down. We need to talk about this."

"What's there to talk about?" Nadia glared on me. "I wake up around strangers, and one of them suddenly turns into a monster and tries to kill me. Sound familiar?"

I remembered with a jolt that Nadia had been unconscious since the farmhouse. She knew nothing about this place. All the trauma and fear we'd suffered together was fresh in her memory.

"It's not like that," I replied, my voice weak. "These are good people."

"I'm leaving." Nadia's voice rang out, clear and certain. "And you should come with me. Please, Sarah. Let's go *home*."

Tears welled up in my eyes as I stared at her. I didn't know what to do anymore. Seeing Lucian as an out-of-control beast had horrified me, but I also knew it couldn't have come out of nowhere. Some shifter instinct had made him snap... something about Nadia.

If Nadia *wasn't* his mate, then who was?

Dymitri had shifted when he'd seen me, but he hadn't wanted to kill me; quite the opposite in fact. He'd been in complete control, desperate to seduce me but not without my cooperation in that fact. So, what had happened to Lucian for this to occur?

I frowned. When Dymitri had described the sorceress's vision, he'd seemed so certain about both of us. When I'd asked Cass about it, she'd agreed that Marienne had never been wrong before.

But everything was starting to add up. Lucian's cold demeanor around me and the way he seemed to have withdrawn from Dymitri since I'd arrived, even though the two of them had always been close.

"We should wait," I said.

"For *what?*" Nadia shook her head. "Come on, no one's guarding the doors. We have to get out while we still can!"

I opened my mouth to protest further, but before I could say anything, the sound of glass shattering from an upstairs window made us both scream and dive for the floor. Another crash of broken glass, this time closer, set cold air rushing over our bodies.

Oh, no. What was that? Did one of them escape the castle? That wasn't good.

"Nadia! Oh, my God!" I clutched my sister's hand, and we raced each other to the front door.

I glanced at the scene unfolding at the top of the stairs. Lucian and Dymitri twisted and rolled over one another, locked in battle on the hallway floor. Dymitri was trying desperately to stop Lucian from continuing his rampage of destruction, though I didn't know if he could do it. Not alone.

Where was Damon? Surely, he could step in and help Dymitri. These were his brothers, after all.

While I debated whether to start searching for Damon, Cass or in fact, anyone who might be able to assist, Nadia pulled open the front doors. A blast of chilly air hit me.

I spun around. "Nadia. No!"

But it was too late. My sister was fleeing down the castle stairs and out into the snow. Freezing air swept in. Behind me, the huge window, where the colored dragons had once danced through a glassy sky, lay in pieces on the floor. Bits of glass crunched under my boots as I headed for the doors, breaking into a run.

I didn't have a choice now. I had to follow her. The last time I didn't go after her, she'd almost died. I couldn't have that happen again.

"Nadia, come back!"

I chased her over the drawbridge, and through the narrow, winding streets of town. She was running in a hurried zigzag, like a scared rabbit, not paying attention to where she was going in her terror.

She knocked into food carts and market stalls, barreled

through astonished onlookers, and carried on without stopping. She ran all the way to the narrow track that led out of the village and across the flat, barren wilderness that stretched as far as the eye could see.

"Nadia." I almost reached her, and tried to grab a hold of her, but she shrugged me off, continuing forward with her jaw set and her eyes narrowed. Her cheeks were streaked with dried tears. "Please," I begged. "You'll freeze. It's going to be dark soon. We have to go back."

"I'm not going back there." Nadia sniffed. Her bare toes curled against the snow-covered track, and I winced. "I'm going home."

I jumped in front of her and pushed my hands out, trying to stop her. She had no idea where we were, or just how far from home we really were. "You don't even know where home is from here."

"We're bound to run into a car eventually," she said, wrapping her arms around her chest. The jacket I'd given her covered her hands, making her look even younger than she was. "Seriously, you've been here this whole time?"

"I have." I ducked my head as I fell into step beside her. "I've been waiting for you to get better, so we could go home."

I thought back to the argument Dymitri and I had earlier, and my cheeks burned. The cold wind sliced into my face, and I pulled up the collar of my sweater. Now that I said it out loud, it sounded like a weak excuse.

It's not like I've sat by her bedside this whole time, waiting for her to wake up.

I shoved away the traitorous thought.

We were silent as we continued our trek. The terrain underfoot was getting rockier, and the sky overhead darkened by the minute. I wanted to turn back, but I sensed that Nadia wouldn't have any of it.

She would have to be freezing. Her poor feet must be numb by now.

I shivered, the clothes I wore not suitable for the cold air without my jacket.

"What were those things?" Her small voice broke through the stillness.

Inhaling a shaky breath, I answered her honestly. "Dragons."

I saw her eye-roll coming from a million miles away. "Very funny."

"I'm not joking." I waited until she caught my eye, and her expression sobered. "They're men who turn into dragons, and they're from a royal bloodline. Dymitri never really explained it beyond that. I'm not sure they even know how it works."

Nadia was quiet and my heart thumped as I watched the cogs turn in her head, putting the pieces together. The ancient, lavish castle she'd woken up in. The huge wings, the claws. The wardrobe engulfed in icy flames.

When she finally spoke, however, her question surprised me.

"You said that name before, back in that room. Dymitri." She nudged into my shoulder. "Who is he?"

I bit my lip, taking my time before answering her question. "He was there when I woke up. He thinks we're meant to be together."

Nadia snorted. "Like fate, and all that crap?"

"Actually..." My mouth twisted into a chagrined smile. "It's exactly like that, yeah."

"That's some crazy Stockholm Syndrome you've got there." Nadia shoved her hands into the pockets of my jacket. "Seriously, you meet a guy, he tells you he loves you and you don't ask any other questions? The Sarah I know would *never* have acted like that."

"That's not..." My cheeks burned.

I didn't know how to make her understand. My feelings for

Dymitri ran deep, but I could barely understand them myself, let alone talk about them out loud.

"It's not like that," I said eventually. "He's a good man. He was trying to protect us earlier, Nadia."

"I know what I saw back there," Nadia replied. "Two out-of-control monsters fighting. I don't care what you think he is—he's no different from the one who tried to kill us."

I sighed, with no idea what to say in response.

We continued on in silence. But with every step we took, the panic in my chest twisted tighter and tighter. The castle was nothing but a dark, murky expanse on the bare horizon behind us now.

I can't abandon her, and I can't convince her to come back to the castle with me. We're stuck.

What the hell am I going to do?

By the time I finally managed to persuade Nadia to stop, a howling wind had picked up in the shallow ravine in which we found ourselves.

The snow, which had started off light enough, brushing our shoulders like icing sugar, began to fall faster and thicker. Every direction was a haze of swirling whiteness; it didn't matter which way we turned, everything looked the same. We had no way of knowing which direction the castle lay.

At some point I'd forced Nadia to put on my boots, because her feet were cut and bleeding from walking so long without shoes. I cursed loudly as I struggled over the rocky terrain in my socks.

Now it was my feet almost numb with cold, and I began to worry about frostbite. Or worse.

My heart hammered with terror and disorientation.

We are in so much trouble.

When Nadia's hand slackened in mine, I tightened my grip in alarm. If I lost her out here, we might never find each other.

But she was signaling toward something. Blinking back the driving snow, I made out a shallow crevice in the rocks up ahead, large enough for two people to wriggle into.

It was the only chance of shelter that had presented itself. Staying outside in these conditions would get us nowhere; our only chance was to stay put somewhere sheltered, like this small crevice, and hope that the snow eased up enough that we could get our bearings.

Or maybe Dymitri will find us. I tucked the stray thought away. Given he was probably still in battle with his brother, that scenario was unlikely.

Nadia curled up around me once we were inside the tiny shelter. Her head dropped onto my shoulder, and within a couple of minutes she was asleep.

Was that a good thing? I had read somewhere about not going to sleep in the snow, but she had literally just woken up from a long illness. Perhaps I should leave her to sleep for a while?

I tugged my jacket around the both of us as best I could.

How did this happen? It seemed like minutes ago, I was in Dymitri's arms in the heat of the hot springs cave, safe, warm, and protected.

Loved.

Now, we were miles away from the castle, trapped in what was fast becoming a blizzard of epic proportions. At least in this tiny crevice, we were shielded from the worst of it.

Nadia snuggled closer to me, letting out a soft breath. I could feel her heartbeat against mine and cuddled her close. She wasn't a baby anymore. She was nineteen, but still, I could remember what it was like to hold her when she was really young.

She was still weak, and despite how incredibly stupid it had been to walk this far in the snow, tears gathered in my eyes for how grateful I was to have her alive, and with me. I'd been so close to losing her forever.

I pressed my face against the top of her head. Despite everything, I couldn't blame her for reacting the way she had in her fragile, traumatized state. I could imagine how it had looked to her. How it *sounded.* If I were in her shoes, I might have fled just as fast.

My thoughts drifted back to the castle.

What if Lucian has totally lost control? It might take Dymitri all night to calm him down. If he is able to, at all. What if Lucian hurt Dymitri? What if he... No. Don't think the worst.

My toes curled up in the thick socks. At least, I think they did. It was hard to tell, as my whole feet were numb from all the time we'd spent out here in the frozen weather.

I don't think we'll last all night out here.

I tried to distract myself by wondering what the sorceress had in mind for Lucian. If Nadia wasn't his mate, then who was? *Sisters.*

A thought glowed in the back of my mind. A fragment of conversation, something Dymitri had said.

You probably have shifter ancestry in your bloodline, if you go back far enough.

A realization began to form in my mind. Something that was so obvious, now that I looked at it, I wondered why I hadn't thought of it before.

If we ever made it through this night alive, and I found my way back to Dymitri, I would let him know. *I wonder...*

I DIDN'T KNOW how much time had passed.

All I knew was that it was pitch black. The wind howled over the rocks above us, and the occasional blast of snow made me squeeze my eyes shut tight against the cold.

The night seemed endless. The storm raged on around us, huge and unstoppable. Nadia and I were just two tiny specks in the face of such a vast and untamable beast.

I'm sorry, sister. I've failed you. I've failed both of us.

Weirdly, I didn't feel as cold as I had before. A lazy warmth was burrowing its way through my bones like a thick blanket. My eyelids were heavy; I wanted desperately to close them, to go to sleep for just a second...

My eyes snapped open. A single thought struck through my mind, clear and simple: *If you go to sleep, you'll die.*

I pulled my sister closer to share our body heat and forced myself to stay awake. My thoughts immediately went to Dymitri, and what had passed between us during this time.

I'd fallen in love with him, and that hadn't been in my plans. Not at all. A month ago I'd been a college student, wanting to party, and study, and have fun while I was young. But then we'd been taken, and every breath had been painful. At times I'd wanted it all to be over. Just so I could get away from the tragedy of what had become of us.

And then we'd been given a second chance at life. Or at least, *I* had been. And while I was with Dymitri, all my college plans had seemed stupid. Small in the bigger scheme of things.

I'd had a dragon prince rescue me and want to be with me forever. What more could there be in this world than to be with him? If I really was honest with myself, all I wanted to do was love Dymitri, and make him feel needed. He'd never had that, and he deserved it. I wanted to give him a baby, who would adore him as much as I did.

And if I got another chance, I'd tell him all of this. That I was his. And he was mine. And despite everything, family obligation, my plans, nothing else mattered now.

The more my thoughts wandered, the more I struggled to remember why that would be such a bad thing. My limbs were stiff, and my thoughts were sluggish, weighed down by the snow and cold.

I sent a silent prayer out to the world. There was nothing we could do now; our only hope of rescue came from the man whose love I had turned away mere hours ago.

My eyelids drooped as my vision became hazy. With every ounce of strength I had left in me, I repeated one thing in my mind, again and again. *Dymitri. Please... we're here. Come find us!*

ELEVEN

DYMITRI

The wind howled down through the shattered window above us.

I stood over my brother, glaring down on him. We had shifted back to human, and our chests heaved with residual anger. Twin furies simmered in the air between us, and for a hot second, I thought he was going to get up and take another swing at me, this time in human form.

But he didn't. His head slumped down against his chest, face falling into shadow.

"She's not my mate, brother." Lucian's voice was broken with despair. "When I looked at her... I... I felt *nothing*."

I dropped my gaze, my chest twisting. It had always been the same way between us: Lucian's sorrow was my sorrow; his happiness was my happiness. This was all wrong. We should be celebrating the recovery of his mate right now...

Instead, both Sarah and Nadia were gone. Vanished.

By the time Lucian had calmed down enough to shift back, dusk was gathering, and long shadows crept toward us over the marble floor.

I cast my eye around at the destruction we'd wrought on our brother's castle. We were surrounded by a mass of broken shards.

"I know," I whispered. "I'm sorry."

"How could the sorceress have been wrong?" Lucian met my eyes. Now all the rage and destruction had passed, I saw him for what he was. What he'd always been. My little brother. Grieving for something that had never existed at all. "You and Sarah…"

"She's my mate," I said, my voice firm. "But she wants to leave. So, it looks like we'll both be alone after all."

My bitter voice echoed off the cold stone. Lucian rose to his feet, shaking his head.

"No." He tilted his chin up. "You hear me? No. We're going to get them back. *Both* of them."

"You don't have to help me do that."

"Yes, I do." Lucian wiped a hand over his face before surveying the chaos around us. "I owe you that much. They left because of me."

I didn't have an answer for that. He wasn't wrong, after all.

"I'm not going to endanger your happiness any more, just because I haven't found mine." Lucian's eyes were like shards of ice as they stared past me, out through the open doors where snow had begun to fall. "Let's find them, and bring them back alive."

LUCIAN and I took to the air.

Flying in tandem like this again, it was like things were back where they should be. With Lucian by my side, I soared up toward the cloud banks that scudded high above the uppermost towers, circling around so I could look at the ground spread out far below us.

Even with full winter gear, this terrain was dangerous for two human women. On foot, there was only one track that led from the village below the castle; they wouldn't have had any option but to follow it.

I turned into a graceful spiral and dived through the air, dropping close to the ground to see if I could pick up their trail. Lucian followed me, right at my shoulder as always.

Fighting him had gone against every instinct I had, but in some ways, I was glad for it. Now the air between us was clearer, and we were on the same page again.

Lucian shifted course slightly as the road narrowed. Shallow, rocky outcrops sprouted up below us, snaking toward a dip in the landscape.

I had a good mental map of the terrain; Damon had shown us the king's lands from the air and on foot, and we were used to tracking our enemies over both.

But this was different. This was Sarah—and she was in danger. I could *feel* it.

I followed Lucian as we flew. The sun had vanished below the horizon and both the wind and snow had picked up. The weather and the cold got worse, and worse, until the storm was raging around us.

Sarah! My mind screamed for her. *Where are you?*

All around us, thick snowflakes whirled in icy droves. The wind battered our wings and darkness threatened to drown everything out. We pushed on through it all, searching through the storm, to no avail.

Sarah!

We couldn't give up. If we couldn't find them in time, they would both die.

Up ahead, the swirling blackness gave way. I spotted a faint light. It was nothing more than a blur at first, and I thought I was seeing things. But it didn't go away. It just hovered there, like a bright beacon.

I started toward the light. I met Lucian's eyes in the darkness. His gaze was blank; he hadn't seen anything.

But he trusted me, so we headed in that direction.

The light was coming from a shallow cave. It was little more than a crevice in the rockface, scarcely big enough for one person, let alone two.

But when I ducked my head, my heart almost stopped inside my chest.

Nadia and Sarah lay curled up around one another. I landed and nudged Sarah's shoulder, but she was unconscious.

At least, that was what I told myself. After everything we'd gone through together, I couldn't contemplate the alternative.

I leaned in and clawed my way through the stone, knocking aside a boulder, and pulled the two bodies from the wreckage. They were like rag dolls in my grasp, limp and icy.

My heart thudded with fear as I clutched Sarah close to my chest.

Please, let her be alive. Oh, God... please. I can't lose her. Not like this. If she wants to go home, so be it. But not like this.

Lucian took Nadia from me. We both inhaled deeply, letting our chests fill with smoldering warmth before we clutched their limp forms against us. For now, it was the best we could do to keep them warm, until we could get them back to the castle.

I stared into the black sky while the blizzard continued to howl around us. I pulled Sarah close with my claws and extended my wings out.

As one, Lucian and I launched ourselves into the air and flew the women home, to our brother's castle.

～

Sarah

My dreams were muddled and hazy. I'd been dipping in and out of them for what seemed to be an eternity, hovering in the space between sleep and wakefulness.

In one dream, I was back home, and my parents were talking in the next room. In another, I was at college. At one point, I had a nightmare. I was back in the basement, Nadia slumped beside me. And this time, it was my fault. It was *all* my fault...

When I finally came back to reality, a hand was holding mine, warm and soft. I gripped the fingers like they were a lifeline.

"Sarah...."

Hearing Dymitri's whispered voice, I turned my head to peer at him through half-opened eyelids. His other hand came up to cradle my fingers.

"You're awake."

Déjà vu. We've been here before.

I squeezed his hand again, harder this time.

"Ouch," he said. He didn't look hurt, though. With my human strength, I probably hadn't affected him at all.

"Sorry." I scrunched my face at the sound of my own voice. It was so thin and raspy, like I'd been crawling through a desert. *The irony.* "Just checking you're real, that's all."

"I'm real." His eyes were soft, and full of relief. "For a little while there, I thought I might lose you."

Nadia! I sucked in a quick breath. "My sister?"

Dymitri nodded. "She's fine. Recovering, like you, but she'll be okay."

I sagged with relief, then, with his help, I struggled upright. He shoved a couple more pillows behind my head until I was only half-reclined. I felt kind of stupid, but I let him fuss over me. It felt nice to have someone who cared that much.

"I'm not going anywhere," I said. "I promise."

He looked up sharply, taking in the weight of my words. We

stared at each other for a long moment. We were alone. There were no other priorities. No distractions. Just the two of us.

"Do you mean that?" He lowered his gaze. "Because if you don't..."

"I do," I told him honestly. "When we were in that storm, I thought we were going to die. I had a lot of time to think about life. About what I wanted."

I took his face in my hands, tilting his head toward me. "Dymitri, it's you. You're what I want. I couldn't stop thinking about you... what I'd be letting go if I just walked away and went back to my old life." I pushed my forehead against his, inhaling softly. That delicious scent, always there to entice me. "I'm not sure I *can* walk away."

I felt the familiar rumble of his voice through my body when he answered. "I meant what I said, Sarah. I'd never hold you against your will. When you ran... I thought of how you must see me. A vicious beast. A monster." His voice turned fierce. "I'm not like those men who kept you in that basement, Sarah. With me, you'll always have a choice."

"I know." I pressed a kiss to his forehead. "And if we're really doing this, I need you to accept me. All of me. The human world will always be part of that."

"I can live with that." His face broke into a smile. "And to think, until recently, I'd never been south of the mountains."

I thought of all the things I wanted to do with him. Take him to the city, to my college. Introduce him to the rest of my family. Maybe we could have a road trip. My heart soared with the possibilities.

"You're not the only one caught between two worlds, Sarah." In a gesture that was now familiar to me, Dymitri tucked a loose strand of hair behind my ear. "My father never accepted me. For the longest time, I thought King Damon was my enemy. Even now, I walk these hallways wondering if everyone sees me the way I see myself—the bastard son of a tyrant."

He glanced toward the window, as if it was difficult for him to meet my gaze. I shifted closer, taking his hand and pulling him properly onto the bed. He came willingly, joining me under the mass of blankets.

"But you taught me that I was enough," he said. His arms slid down to my waist. I was still warm with sleep, but I shivered under his touch, nevertheless. "Everything—the good and the bad. Thanks to you, I can finally see a future for myself here."

I surged forward, catching his mouth with mine. He kissed me back passionately, tangling his hands in my hair. Before I could deepen the kiss, however, he pulled back.

"Wait," he panted, ignoring my frustrated whine. "Does this mean... you'll stay forever? You'll mate with me?"

"Yes." I pressed kisses everywhere on him I could reach. I burned with want, eager for his touch. "*Yes*. I'm yours, Dymitri."

His eyes darkened, and he let out an inhuman growl.

"That's right." His voice dropped even lower than usual. "You're mine."

I'd heard that growl once before, by the fireside. Then, it had frightened me enough that I ran to the other side of the castle.

Now, I felt the folds between my legs becoming wet and slick with anticipation.

He leaned into me and tightened his grip on my waist, pulling me into his lap. I slid my knees onto either side of him, rocking into his already hard length. I groaned as his cock pressed up against me, shivers of pleasure racing through my body.

It was the work of a moment for him to slide off my nightgown. Feeling my naked body against his clothed one was amazing, but I wanted to taste his bare skin. Without pausing, I pulled open his shirt halfway and began pressing open-mouthed kisses to his flesh.

You don't understand, I thought wildly. *You're* mine, *just as much as I'm yours.*

Once he shoved off his clothes, we came together again, twisting and rolling as our bodies slid together in ecstasy. He pinned me underneath him, holding my arms up against the headboard. I whined with need and arched against him as one of his huge hands bracketed my wrists. The other drifted down-wards, toying with my nipple.

I bucked up again, grinding my hips into his until we both groaned.

"I need you inside me. Dymitri, *please.*"

His eyes darkened even further, and his lips came down onto mine as he lined himself up. He slid into me in one smooth stroke. I moaned and pushed back against him as much as I could, and he met my hips with his own, rutting into me over and over.

This wasn't like before. Before, our joining had been delicate and soft... almost sweet.

Now, it was a true claiming. I was his mate, and he was making me his own. I submitted to it willingly, taking everything he had to give, my body opening up around his cock like it was made just for him. Perhaps it was.

He surrounded me completely, covering my body with his as he made love to me. His hands slid down to my hips and pulled them higher so he could get a deeper angle, and I whimpered as he found my g-spot, my fingers clawing uselessly at the bedsheets. I was going to come soon; I could feel it building up inside me, like the crest of a wave, forceful and inevitable.

"Mine." He sucked at my bare neck as he continued to thrust relentlessly.

"Yours," I gasped out.

He released a low groan and I felt his cock pulse as he filled me with his seed. My pussy tightened around him at the realization that we were unprotected—he could be making me pregnant, right here and right now.

I couldn't hold it back anymore. The thoughts of everything our future might hold sent me tumbling over the edge, and wave after wave of pleasure crashed through my body. Dymitri fucked me through it, still pumping me full, and I took it all gladly.

When we finally collapsed beside one another, my head swam with happiness. I pressed a hand to my belly, letting out a long sigh.

All I wanted to do now was drift off to sleep. Safe and warm and replete in the arms of my mate.

TWELVE

SARAH

I must have fallen asleep, because too soon I woke to the sound of Dymitri shutting the door and re-entering the room.

I sat up in bed and smiled at him. "Hey. Where'd you go?"

"I went to check on your sister, and she's awake. Which is great."

I threw back the blankets and jumped out of bed. "I want to see her. Can we go now?"

Dymitri nodded, his jaw tight. "I think we all need to."

I frowned, not quite understanding. "Who's we?"

"Lucian and I. He wants to apologize to her, and sort things out between them. The castle has been very tense since our fight."

I bit my lip, then nodded. "Okay. But I'll word Nadia up first. She's only nineteen and has always been a little afraid of big men like your brother."

I pulled on the fresh clothes laid out for me on the side table, shivering with the coolness in the air. We'd been so cold in that small crevice, it gave me chills just thinking about it now.

"I'll take you to Nadia, then go and get Lucian. There's a lot to discuss."

I didn't ask what he meant. My only concern was getting to Nadia as soon as possible and seeing her alive and well again.

I'd really thought we were going to die out in the wilderness. Frozen to death, never to be seen again.

When I opened the door to her bedroom, Nadia jumped up from the bed. "Sarah!"

She raced for me, and I swept her up in my arms, holding her tight.

"I am so sorry." She sobbed against me, her small frame shuddering. "We almost died. And it's all my fault."

I pulled back from her and grabbed her hands. "Nadia, listen to me. You were terrified and had no idea where you were. Then those two brothers turned into dragons. Trust me, I know why you ran. I would have done the same thing the day I met them, if it wasn't for the fact that you were still unconscious and I had to wait for you to wake up."

Nadia brushed the tears from her cheeks. "Well... you did have another reason to stay."

I smiled and straightened up. "Dymitri."

I glanced behind me. He hadn't arrived yet. I took her hand and tugged her to the windowsill so we could speak quietly together.

"He's the one I want to be with, Nadia. I'm sorry I didn't get a chance to properly explain it all to you. Before."

She smiled softly at me. "It's okay. I understand."

I gripped her hand and squeezed her fingers. "You probably can't understand, but please know, he makes me so happy. I am totally in love with him."

She laughed. "I know. I can see it all over your face."

The guys were coming, their footsteps echoing in the hallway. "Then please trust me when I say, these men are good people."

The door opened and Dymitri stuck his head in. "Do you two want to join us for a drink in the dining hall?"

I jumped to my feet. "That's a great idea. We'll be right there."

Dymitri shut the door again and I couldn't help but smile at how thoughtful he was being.

"What's that about?" Nadia asked, already grabbing her coat.

"Lucian wants to apologize for what happened."

"Oh."

I slid my hand into the crook of her elbow and gently directed her out of the bedroom, and into the hallway. "He feels terrible about it. So please... just let him apologize, hun."

"Okay."

I led my sister to the dining hall, though I could feel her reticence. As far as she was concerned, these two men were monsters. I just happened to be in love with one of them.

The fire was blazing in the grate, and Dymitri sat with his brother at the table, waiting for us.

"Hot chocolates?" he asked, gesturing to the table where hot drinks were waiting, along with platters of sweets.

"Thank you," I said, sitting down and grabbing for a drink. "I'm famished."

I took a long sip of my hot chocolate and sighed as the sweetness ran over my tongue.

Dymitri cleared his throat. Lucian stared at the table, looking worried and slightly sick.

"Go on, brother."

Lucian looked up, his face hard and his jaw tight. "I need to apologize to you both, for my abhorrent behavior. I am... ashamed to have scared you in the way that I did."

Nadia gulped. "Oh. Lucian, I..."

"No," he said fiercely, shaking his head. "You both could have died, and that would have been my fault. If I'd only retained control over my dragon, none of this would have happened."

I glanced over at Nadia, whose eyes were filling with tears.

"It's okay. Really," I said. "You weren't in your right mind."

Lucian shook his head. "No, I was not."

Nadia stared at him. "Isla told me you saved me from those men back at the farm. You brought me here. You saved my life."

Lucian looked at her, his eyes wide and fearful. "Yes. But then I—"

"Why did you freak out like that?" she asked suddenly. "Was it something I said? Or did?"

"No! It was…" Lucian sighed, running a hand through his long dark hair and pushing it off his face. "I was ashamed. And angry. I'd been told you were my fated mate, but I don't feel those things for you that Dymitri obviously feels for Sarah."

"And when I woke up, I confirmed it was true, didn't I?" Nadia asked gently. "That I wasn't your soul mate."

He nodded, his throat working as he swallowed his pain. "Yes, and I… we…"

Dymitri cleared his throat loudly. "My brother and I have grown up in the wilderness, together. Only recently have we been welcomed back into the castle, and our feelings of abandonment and pain have not gone away."

Nadia wiped at a tear that had fallen on her cheek. "I'm so sorry I hurt you."

I reached over and touched my sister's arm. "It's not your fault. Fated mates are created, born for each other. Neither Lucian, nor you, chose this. And it's no one's fault."

"Except Marienne's." Lucian growled.

I laughed. I couldn't help it. "Yes! Let's shoot the messenger."

Dymitri frowned at me in disapproval, and I waved my hand at him.

"It's just a human joke. Oh, forget about it." I turned to Nadia. "They were told by a fortune teller, of sorts, that we were their mates. By a sorceress called Marienne. She was right about me and Dymitri, but unfortunately, she was wrong about you two."

A smile quivered on Nadia's lips. "Well, one out of two isn't bad."

I glanced across at Dymitri. "I'm grateful for it."

Nadia stood up and reached for Lucian's arm. "Can you stand up? I need to hug you."

"What for?" he asked, though he got to his feet anyway.

"For saving my life." Nadia pressed herself into the huge dragon's chest.

His eyes went wide, and worried, then he softened, wrapping his arms around her.

A soft sigh filled the air and I smiled at my mate.

"I never had a little sister before," Lucian whispered.

I grinned as Nadia pulled back and stared up at Lucian. "And I never had a brother before."

They settled back into their seats and the atmosphere in the room buzzed with energy.

"Now that that's settled, Nadia, we have a question for you," Dymitri said, his deep voice booming in the room.

"We do?" I asked him.

He smiled at me, then focused on my sister. "Would you like to stay here, with us? In the winter palace? Damon and Cass have said you can both stay, for as long as you like."

My heart dropped in my chest, and I turned to my sister.

Nadia stared at me with a similar type of anguish.

"You're staying?" she whispered.

Tears welled in my eyes, burning the back of my throat. "I have to. I can't leave Dymitri."

Nadia nodded. "I knew that, but to hear it..." She wiped at the tears that dropped onto her cheeks. "I'm going to miss you so much."

"Stay," I whispered. "Please. There's no reason for you to leave."

Nadia glared at me. "No reason? Sarah, I have college, and my friends. Mom and Dad!"

I pressed my lips together, pain ricocheting through my chest. "I know."

She put out her hand to me. "I'll tell them all you met the guy of your dreams and can't possibly leave him."

I laughed, choking on the sound. "That's pretty close to the truth."

I got to my feet and pulled my little sister into my arms for a hug.

Dymitri said from behind me, "We'll organize a way to get you home, Nadia."

I closed my eyes. I didn't want to think about her leaving me, but it was my turn to focus on my future. And my future was here. With my dragon prince.

I finally understood what true bliss felt like: having my mate, holding her safe in my arms, her head resting softly on my shoulder as we drifted in the afterglow of our love-making.

The morning sunlight shone through our window. Faint noises echoed down distant hallways, and the clatter of plates downstairs told me that breakfast was almost ready.

I didn't care. I wanted to stay here forever, just like this.

But reality came knocking on the door sooner rather than later.

I groaned, throwing a pillow in the direction of the door, but the hammering increased.

"Dymitri!" Cass's muffled, irate voice came through the wood. "I know you're in there! Come on!"

Sarah frowned sleepily and looked up at me. "What's that all about?"

"It's time to take your sister back to the human world."

Sarah sat upright in bed. A faint look of dismay crossed her beautiful features. It had been three days since we'd had our talk in the dining hall, though I'm sure Sarah had deliberately put it out of her head, hoping this day would never come.

"You must have known this was coming." I kept my voice soft. I hated to hurt her in any way. "She doesn't want to stay here, my love. And we can't keep her if she doesn't wish it."

"No, I know." Sarah drew up her shoulders before letting out a long sigh. "I just... I'll miss her. That's all. She's my baby sister. I'll always worry about her."

I gathered Sarah up in my arms. "I understand. She's much better, though. She can travel now."

"Okay." Sarah sighed, and we begrudgingly tugged on some clothes and headed downstairs.

We were the last ones down to breakfast. A chorus of smiling faces greeted us, ranging from genuinely happy grins from Damon and Cass, to knowing smirks from our siblings, Lucian and Nadia.

We took our seats, and my stomach lurched with hunger. I was starving.

I didn't care what the others thought about our lazy hours in bed. Sarah was mine. I wanted the whole world to know it.

Nadia and Sarah sat at one end of the table, speaking in quiet voices, their heads close. Cass sat next to them, with Damon at the head of the table. Lucian was on the other side, sitting a little apart from the others.

Lucian's apology to Nadia, along with him saving her life, seemed to have changed her perspective on dragon shifters. Since yesterday, she'd let Cass drag her around on a tour of the castle, and even expressed an interest in some of the rare herbs and mushrooms that the village market had to offer.

So far, she'd flat-out refused to actually *ride* on the back of a dragon, however. Which might pose something of a problem when the time came to take her home.

I nudged my brother in the back of the head, and he scowled

at me. When Nadia had initially woken up and we realized she wasn't his mate, he'd torn the palace apart in his frustrations.

But now he seemed to have accepted the fact, and he'd brightened up considerably since realizing he wasn't broken. She just wasn't the one for him. He'd even suggested that he could be the one to take her home, but I turned him down.

I needed to make sure Sarah's sister got back safely. I wanted to be the one to tell her family she was okay.

"Is it time?" Nadia's voice broke through my thoughts. I realized she and Sarah were both standing up at the table, looking at me.

"It's time."

The morning air was crisp and bright, the perfect conditions for flying—not too windy, and a clear sky for navigation. Cass, Damon, and Lucian joined us in the cobblestoned courtyard as Sarah and Nadia hugged each other tightly.

"I love you," Sarah said, face muffled against her sister's shoulder. "We'll see each other again soon, okay? Tell Mum and Dad and Katerina that I love them."

Nadia sniffled and laughed as she pulled away, wiping her tears with her sleeve. "Katerina won't believe a word of this, will she?"

"Probably not." Sarah looked close to tears as well, but she was holding it together for now.

"Wait." Cass frowned. "Who the hell is Katerina?"

"Oh..." Nadia raised an eyebrow at Sarah before turning to the rest of us. "Right. Sorry. She's our older sister. We don't see her that often, but she'll come back home for this, I'm sure of it."

My heart flipped over in my chest.

Another sister?

The conversation moved on quickly, but I couldn't stop turning it over in my mind, and wondering...

Sarah

I watched Nadia and Dymitri soar high into the sky, Nadia's shrieks piercing my ears until they were out of earshot.

She hadn't wanted to get on the dragon's back, but the other option was being held in Dymitri's claws. To Nadia, riding on his back was the lesser of the two evils.

The silhouette of Dymitri's huge wings covered the sun. My heart ached. I knew I'd be returning home soon to see her again—Dymitri had promised that I would be able to traverse between the worlds on occasion—but tears still blurred my vision. I watched them until they were nothing but a pinprick on the horizon.

Cass and I returned to breakfast together. My appetite had vanished, and I sank back into my chair with a heavy heart.

"Do you want to walk through the maze after breakfast?" Cass's unusually soft tone broke me out of my thoughts. "Or we could get the cooks to make something sweet."

"I'm fine," I replied automatically. My shoulders hunched inwards, and I sighed. "I'm... I'm worried about her. I can't help feeling like..."

Cass tilted her head to one side. "Like what?"

"Like I'm being selfish." I let my head thud back against the heavy oak chair. "All this... It's wonderful. I want to be here, with Dymitri, but she's my sister. What if she needs me?"

"Nadia is a grown woman. She can make her own choices. And *you*," she said, prodding my shoulder, "deserve to be happy. Life is short. You need to grab happiness with both hands and live it. Fated mates don't come around every day, trust me."

At the head of the table, Damon grinned. He put his hand on Cass's and tangled their fingers together. The gesture was sweet, and surprising from the king who wasn't known for being outwardly affectionate to anyone other than his wife.

"She's right, you know," he told me, eyes twinkling.

I tipped my head back and laughed. "Thanks, guys."

The pep talk hadn't fixed everything, but the knot of guilt in my chest eased slightly.

Cass was right. There was no point in worrying about what could have been, or what I should have done better in the past. Life would carry on regardless, and Dymitri was part of my life. Now, and forever.

A soft beam of sunlight hit my face, and I basked in the warmth of it. Dymitri would be back soon. I wasn't a shifter, but the love in my heart in that moment could have rivalled that of any dragon.

And, if I can't hold onto anything else... I can hold onto that.

EPILOGUE

SARAH

A month later

"You look amazing." Nadia grinned widely, her gaze running up and down my body. She held a bouquet of trailing holly, ivy, and winter roses in her hands—the only plants we could find in the garden to cobble together at this time of year. "A true dragon princess."

I rolled my eyes, fighting back a blush. "It's too much, isn't it?"

"Definitely not." Katerina reached over to rearrange the bouquet a little, pulling out some wilting flowers here and there. "This is your wedding, Sarah! You have to look the part."

I glanced down at myself, smoothing out the gauzy fabric of my skirt. The dress was simple, but it was topped off by a long fur-lined cloak. I flushed happily and accepted the flowers from Nadia.

"Oh, I almost forgot." Nadia picked up a delicate circlet that Cass had given to me as an early wedding gift and fitted it over my hair. "*Now* you're ready."

"You know..." Katerina reached down to adjust the back of the coat as I stepped up to the doorway. "It's okay if you want to post-pone. We can still call it off."

She made a muffled sound of pain, like Nadia had stepped on her foot.

"What? It's kind of soon to be marrying this guy, sis. I'm just saying."

"They're eloping!" Nadia retorted. "It's *romantic,* Kat."

"Shh!" I hissed, and they fell silent. Inwardly, I rolled my eyes. *Sisters.*

The guards on either side of the doorway clicked their heels, and the doors opened. I smiled when I saw the tall candles deco-rated with ivy and roses. Cass had refused to be a bridesmaid with my sisters and decided instead to decorate the hall for our small ceremony.

It didn't bother her that there was no-one here to see it except us. In her mind, even a simple ceremony should be beautiful.

We hadn't wanted to wait, and with my friends being human, and Dymitri being, well, Dymitri, everyone who was important was here anyway.

Except my parents. My father was unwell, and unable to travel. I hadn't wanted to push him, especially with the truth of who I was marrying. A royal dragon shifter from another realm. It had been hard enough to convince Katerina to come, and she didn't even know the extent of everything. I'd taken her to the airport, given her a sleeping tablet for flying, and met Dymitri once Kat fell asleep.

He'd been the one to fly us home, and I still hadn't explained everything to my sister yet. That was a problem for another day.

Today was my wedding day.

"Let's go," I said, nodding at my beautiful sisters.

They both smiled at me, then walked through the doors. I followed them down the aisle.

Damon and Cass stood to one side, their faces glowing with happiness.

Lucian stood beside Dymitri, who waited for me at the end of the small aisle.

My heart lifted as my groom locked eyes with me. His face broke into a smile as I made my way toward him.

"You look incredible," he murmured when I reached him.

I ran my hand over the lapel of his jacket. It was the most dressed up I'd ever seen him. I wondered if Cass was the one who'd gotten him into that suit.

"You don't look so bad yourself," I whispered with a smile.

That was an understatement. His suit fit him perfectly, his broad shoulders tapering down to his waist. I was already thinking about peeling his clothes off him later. My teeth caught on my bottom lip with the thought.

Someone gasped behind me and I turned to see Katerina gaping at Lucian, her mouth open in surprise.

I followed her gaze and caught sight of Lucian's expression. He was standing just behind Dymitri's right shoulder, staring past me.

My heart jumped. He was staring at Katerina, the same way Dymitri stared at me.

Lucian's eyes darkened. His pupils were black in an eerie resemblance to his brother's, and I realized immediately what was happening.

Katerina is his mate.

My sisters and I had been in our own rooms, in another part of the castle, while we prepared for the wedding. Lucian hadn't had a chance to cross paths with her until now.

Marienne wasn't wrong. All this time, my sister *was* Lucian's mate.

But not Nadia.

Katerina.

"I'm sorry…" Lucian muttered into Dymitri's ear.

I was close enough to hear the pain in his words. His hands clenched into fists at his sides, and I realized that he was barely holding it together.

"I… I have to go."

Dymitri turned, and comprehension dawned on his face. "Brother…"

Before Dymitri could touch him, Lucian stumbled back, knocking over one of Cass's floral arrangements. It clattered to the ground but he kept running, almost barreling into Cass herself in his rush to get away.

It was horrible to see him run from his mate when his dragon wanted her so badly, but he strode out of the hall as fast as his legs would carry him.

Katerina gripped my elbow and whispered into my ear. "Who was that?"

I gave her a reassuring smile. "My brother-in-law. I'll explain later."

I had a wedding to get through first.

Dymitri's face was crestfallen as he watched his brother go. I put a hand on his arm, gently drawing his attention back to me.

"Do you want to go after him?" I whispered.

"Shall I proceed?" the minister asked in a low voice, leaning forwards.

Dymitri hesitated.

"It's okay." He caught my eye and took my hand, lacing our fingers together. "Once upon a time, it was just us, Lucian and I. But it looks like he's not going to be alone any longer. And neither am I."

He squeezed my fingers.

My chest filled with warmth as I looked into the eyes of the man I loved.

Dymitri was right. Our families went beyond blood now. I

would always love my sisters, and Dymitri would always love Lucian... but we had our own life to build now. Together.

The trauma in our pasts had made it hard for us to trust each other, but we were beyond that now. I wasn't interested in the past any longer.

It was time to look to the future.

Hand in hand, we turned to the minister, ready to exchange our vows.

THE END

Read on for a sneak peek into book 5 in the *Dragon Kings of Fire and Ice* series.

The Dragon's True Mate

I staggered out of the hall, away from my brother's wedding, and the woman he'd taken as his bride. His fated mate.

Sarah and Dymitri had been right from the very start. From the moment they met, I'd been able to see the intensity of the feelings Dymitri had toward her.

And I'd hoped it would be the same for me and my mate. Marienne had said it would be, only when I met Nadia, it hadn't been. I'd felt nothing except sympathy for Nadia when we'd found her hurt, and unconscious.

When she'd woken up, there had been none of the feelings I'd been promised. No passion. No quivering desire. No dragon raring his possessive head.

The lack of those feelings had sent me into a rage unlike any other. I'd felt so hurt and betrayed. So disappointed. But I'd gotten through it, and hoped to one day find my own mate. Perhaps a servant in the castle. Or one of the women in town.

But no... it was another human woman. Just like my brother.

Not Nadia, but Sarah's other sister. Katerina.

I burst through the doors, my gut tightening to the point of me running bent over.

"Hold it together," I told myself, struggling to hold onto my humanity.

I ran for the front door of the castle, passing by the foyer that had only recently been patched up from my rage-filled tantrum. Dymitri and I had done irreparable damage to the once-grand colored glass windows.

I burst through the front doors, feeling the cold blast of our icy winter breeze on my face.

I reveled in the sensation, breathing in the air.

Calm down, calm down.

My dragon was furious for running away from my mate. He wanted me to go back, but I couldn't. I just couldn't.

I also had no hope of containing him anymore.

I threw my jacket to the ground as my dragon rose up inside of me. Wings sprouted from my back, and my skin became the hardened scales of my shifter.

I closed my eyes and let my mind go as mist swirled up around me, and I became my dragon.

When I opened my eyes, the world around me looked different. But the feelings inside of me weren't.

My mate was here. And Marienne had been right. My fated mate was human, and she was a sister to Sarah. But it hadn't been her tiny, younger sister Nadia.

Instead, my mate was her older sister. The gorgeous, overly curvy Katerina. With her dark curls, and a sexy smile that made my skin catch fire.

I leapt into the air, beating my wings to lift myself high into the sky.

Everything that I'd been told about fated mates was true. My dragon was uncontrollable. My heart was thudding against my chest with the power of a steam train.

Lust poured through me, all for a stranger. A woman who would never understand my world, or our customs.

I'd never been good enough for my father, or any woman I'd known in the past. Why would this gorgeous human woman accept me?

None of it made sense, and in my fury, I couldn't see a way around the problem, except by flying away.

I flew higher and higher, until I couldn't climb anymore, then I soared down, far away from my half-brother's kingdom. Until the sunshine heated my wings, and my winter skin ached from the change in temperature.

There was another kingdom ahead, with a castle perched up in the mountaintops. I could only hope it was Stavrok and Lucy's castle. I'd never been, but had met the royal couple when they'd visited Damon and Cass.

I glanced back the way I'd come. I was weak now, from hunger and fatigue. I'd never make it back. Not tonight. Not now.

I didn't have much of a choice. I used the last of my strength to fly onto a high balcony on one of the castle towers, and collapsed against a railing.

I let my dragon go as a servant ran out to see me, his gaze narrowing as my human body replaced my dragon one.

"Let me get you a robe, sir." He ran off again.

I panted and sighed. I was definitely in the right place. I couldn't imagine anyone in the winter palace treating a stranger so well.

The servant returned with a robe and a glass of water, which I downed immediately.

"Can I help you?" he asked. "Are you here to see King Stavrok?"

I nodded, though it wasn't entirely true. "Could you tell Stavrok and Lucy that I'm here? My name is Lucian. He will know who I am."

The servant bowed and raced off. I managed to stand up and

slide on the robe, just as an older man stepped out onto the balcony.

"Lucian, sir, please follow me."

"Thank you."

I followed the man who had to be the butler into the castle, marveling at the richness of the carpet underfoot, and the grand paintings that lined the halls.

What a difference it made when the king in charge of his kingdom looked after his wealth. Unlike my father, who may have been a king, but was at heart a tyrant.

The worst of men.

~

Book 5 is available now!